VLADISLAV VELKOVSKI

LEGACY
OF THE
NAMELESS

The Epic Journey Of A Troubled Girl

A Legend Of Sitheia
Series, Part One

NORTH ✸ STAR
INVEST LLC

LEGACY OF THE NAMELESS

Copyright © 2021 by Vladislav Velkovski

Written by Vladislav Velkovski

Published by North Star Invest LLC

Contact information:

northstarinvestllc@gmail.com

www.northstarlegends.com

legendofsitheia@gmail.com

First published in 2021

ISBN: 978-1-956255-00-3

Printed in the United States of America

10 9 8 7 6 5 4 3 2 1

DEDICATION

*To my family. For your love,
support and patience.*

CONTENTS

"May your dreams never become dull and mundane."

Vladislav Velkovski

PROLOGUE

My name is Aristobulus and I am a chronicler. I am writing this journal as a way to relieve my aging mind from some of the memories that I have gathered over the roughly two thousand years that I have been alive or something close to being alive.

Also, my assistant has discovered these in her words 'incoherent' notes in several chests up in the attic and she made a point that either I am going to do something with them or she will do something with them at the fireplace.

So I had two choices left to me. Either I had to kill my assistant or I had to write this recollection of my memories and get rid of the notes. I am uncomfortable to say but I really like my assistant. I had trained her for several hundred years and I do not intend to start from the beginning with a new assistant.

I have concluded that she is showing promise that one day after several decades of additional training she might be useful to me. Also she is very caring, bringing me food in my study so I don't have to go eat in the dining hall like the simple fledglings.

Over the centuries I have accumulated so many memories that I had to start writing them down, because I began to fear that one day I will start to lose them. To a younger person's perception it might seem like it is not a big deal to lose a memory or two when you have so many of them.

Unfortunately, most of my vampire family shares that point of view, especially the vampires that are yet to reach their first millennium. It is a common 'knowledge' among vampires that undead beings do not possess a soul.

However, it is my belief and hope that our memories are us and they are the building blocks of a soul. That is where my fear comes from, of letting go of any memories at all.

It would be silly to say that this story that I am about to record is about to start. The true is that this story started more than two thousand years ago before I became one of the undead in a land that used to be a mighty empire. That was long before the vampires and the werewolves came to this land.

History says that it was the greatest empire that ever existed, but when it was at the peak of its power a force from another world intervened. The empire died and its great power shattered and its pieces were hidden in the blood of its descendants.

There was foretelling that these pieces will one day find their way to each other and will reunite. For two thousand years, there was no sign of such an event, until now.

CHAPTER 1

When Sitheia opened her eyes she could hardly see a thing. She couldn't remember a darker night. The moon was hidden and not a single star could be seen from the tick blanket of clouds that covered the sky. Sitheia was shivering in the cold weather. She had no idea what she was doing outside on a night like this with no clothes on.

The heavy rain drenched her skin making her teeth chatter from the cold. Her long brown hair was sticking to her back and neck. Her skin was tingling with goosebumps.

She pushed back the strands that were sticking over her forehead and were covering her eyes. It was difficult to see from the heavy rain and she nearly lost her footing. Looking down, Sitheia noticed that she was standing over a large round rock with a little moss on top of it. It was wet and slick from the rain. Everywhere around her, there were only giant boulders that looked like the crumbled columns from some kind of building. She has never seen a building like that before, except maybe for…

But no, the tower where she has spent most of her youth was too small to produce this much ruble. Besides, only the lower parts of the tower were crumbled. Up the spiral stairs near its top, the tower was just fine and so was the Door.

Sitheia lived in a land where cold weather was not uncommon. But to be outside on a stormy night without clothes was just plain stupid. The thing was that she didn't remember coming out here. And to think of it, where was she? She couldn't see the village or the tower.

She was so cold that she was shivering just like when she had fever when she was little. There was nothing around her but rocks. She hugged herself feeling more alone in the world than ever before.

"Hello!?" She yelled. "Anyone!?"

No one responded. She was alone. There was no one around to share her loneliness with or to make her feel warm. She tried to cry, but the rain did not make that very easy. She was going to die alone, just like before.

A thunder hit somewhere in front of her. The lightning illuminated two forms standing not far from her at a short distance from each other. Spark of hope lit up in her heart. There was someone out there after all. She came closer so she can have a better look. Both of the figures were a lot taller than she was. They were facing each other and seemed to be oblivious of her presence.

Another lightning illuminated them even more and made Sitheia gasp. One face was pale, with red eyes and mouth half opened, with teeth like fangs and hands like claws. He had slick jet black hair and an angry look in his eyes. The other was all hairy and had the appearance of some kind of animal that stood on its hind legs. It had a large mouth like the muzzle of a wolf with big dangerous looking fangs and slime dripping from it.

Sitheia thought that she has never seen any beings prettier than them. Their presence made her feel comfortable and warm. She stopped hugging herself and moved closer. The rain has stopped. Sitheia didn't like that the two figures were angry at each other. She came closer reaching out to touch them, to calm them.

The vampire and the werewolf rushed at each other with angry snarls that made Sitheia wake up.

She woke up discovering that she has somehow fallen asleep at the base of the tower in the middle of a snow covered meadow. She didn't remember coming here at all. It was snowing and she was half buried in the snow.

"How long have I been here?" She said to no one in

particular. After that strange dream she needed to hear someone's voice, anyone's, even if it had to be her own.

Sitheia got up dusting the snow from her clothes. She wasn't dressed for this kind of weather. The winter has officially ended so no one was expecting snow. Still, she thought it a little strange that she has fallen asleep so deep, that she hasn't noticed that she was buried in the snow.

At that moment, Sitheia heard growling. Lifting her eyes Sitheia felt her blood freezing in her veins. The things from her dream were standing few feet away from her. They looked just like in her dream with bared fangs and angry vicious expressions.

The difference from her dream was that now they were not fighting each other, instead they were facing her and they didn't look friendly. Sitheia felt like her feet were made of stone. She couldn't run, she couldn't speak or beg for mercy. All she could do was stare at those angry eyes and those sharp teeth.

Feeling helpless, Sitheia whispered a prayer to the Goddess right before the monsters rushed her.

Her prayer must have been answered because when Sitheia opened her eyes again she was back at her house in her own bed in the bed chamber under the leatherworker shop. It was where she, her little sister, her parents and her grandfather slept. It was a large room where you can place four beds, a table and two wardrobes and there would still be plenty of space for you to move freely without knocking anything.

"Easy, Sitty. Calm down." Her father was holding her arms.

"It's all right, baby. It's all right." Her mother was brushing her face with a wet cloth.

Opening her eyes Sitheia thought 'It was a dream'. She was back in her bed at home.

"What are you doing?" She asked her parents.

"You had a bad dream, honey." Her mother said gently.

"You were screaming and trashing. We had to hold you down, so you wouldn't hurt yourself." Her father said.

With wide open eyes she was looking from one face to the other. Sitheia was horrified. It can't be. She hadn't had one of these 'episodes' in years. Her eyes fell on Dana, her little sister who was watching her from her own bed with a worried expression. She hated making her family worried. Her grandfather had also woken up.

Her parents loosen their grip on her now that they knew that she is aware. Sitheia looked at herself. Her night shirt was a mess. She was so drenched in sweat that it made her feel cold. The memory of the cold rain and the snow from her dream came back to her. She shivered.

"I am sorry I frightened you. I was having a bad dream."

"It's all right, dear." Her mother said with worried

expression that did not help Sitheia feel any better.

"What was the dream about Sitty?" Her father asked.

"It was raining. Also there was a lot of snow and I was alone in the cold. I was scared, that's all I remembered." Sitheia said. She remembered the rest as well, but she didn't want to further worry her parents. Telling anyone about her dreams during one of her 'episodes' never ended well.

"Don't worry sweetie. You are not alone. Your family is here with you." Her father said and both of her parents gave her a hug.

They loved her, her parents. She knew that. But having strange dreams that contradicts with the beliefs of the Cat people made her family concerned that she might be sick in the head and that she needs to be purified.

Sitheia have heard of other cultures where people go to the temples of their deities to worship and ask for guidance or spiritual peace. No one went to the temple of the Goddess unless they had a problem that needed to be fixed. People go there because they are desperately in need of healing. Sick people go to the temple. But if you are not sick and you still need to go to the temple, then something must be wrong with you. At least half of the Cat people could spend their entire life without ever setting a foot inside the temple and the rest may go there once or twice in a lifetime. Unfortunately, Sitheia has been their regular visitor for years.

"No wonder you dreamt that you were out in the rain and you were cold." Her mother said confusing Sitheia. "Look how sweaty you are. You were cold in real life, so you dreamt that you are cold in the dream. Come, change your shirt and go back to bed."

"And honey, just to be sure, you should visit the temple tomorrow." Her father suggested.

CHAPTER 2

Sitheia woke up the next morning feeling exhausted as if she has been climbing a mountain instead of sleeping. The dream that she had last night left her shaken. It felt so real.

And the monsters from her dream. Logic dictated that she should be scared of them, but she wasn't at least not until they attacked her. She felt some kind of strange kinship to them. As if she knew them once, but somehow they have evaporated from her memory and now they were lost to her. Perhaps they were familiar to her from some of her grandpa's stories. Perhaps. It didn't make much sense.

Mary Cat, her mother, would say that she has a very wild imagination. Perhaps she did. On the other hand, the faint memories she had from her grandmother Faith, were of her having dreams that soon after would come true. People called them visions. Sitheia also remembered that every time her grandma would have one of these visions, she also had terrible headaches. Sitheia touched her head just to make sure, but everything seemed to be fine. There was no sign of any headaches. In fact, she felt great, except for being totally rattled by the whole experience of course.

Whatever was the cause for this dream and the resurgence of her 'episodes', Sitheia felt that she has to do something about it. The first thought that came to mind was to go and see the Door at the top of the tower. For most of her life going to see the Door was her go to solution for all of her dilemmas and problems. But, then after a short evaluation of her body she concluded that for some reason she has woken up more tired than when she went to bed and it might be a better idea to go to the temple first to be refreshed.

The temple had a special effect, not only on her, but on everyone. Every time she went there, she felt better afterward. The underground lake filled with enchanted waters that lie under the temple possessed magical properties. People usually went there when they were seriously ill. The healing waters were soothing and they will relax her muscles and she'll be at full strength again. And after visiting the temple, then she can go and see the Door and tell her about her dream.

Sitheia stretched in her bed. As much as she felt like sleeping forever, Sitheia knew that she needs to be getting up. The day was just starting and it wasn't just any ordinary day. It was her birthday. Tonight she will become of age. That was a special moment in the life of any Cat person. Her childhood was officially over and she will have to start being a lot more useful to her family and to the village of Sacred Pools.

Cat. Sitheia often wondered why their people were called the Cat. They had nothing to do with the animal. In the entire village you couldn't find a single cat. There were some wild cats out there, but that was different. Of course, the hunters knew how to move quietly when they were stalking a prey, but there were very few hunters in the village. Apart from her father, there were only a dozen more hunters. And if you looked at the blacksmith or the farmers, they were all huge. There is no way that resemblance was the reason for the name.

Sitheia remembered her grandfather telling her that once the Cat people had a name of their own, long time ago. But, when they made the contract with the Lords of Perdival, that name was forgotten. The name "Cat" they got it from Lord Perdival himself, to protect them.

"Sitty! Wake up! Breakfast!" Her mother yelled from upstairs chasing away any wild thoughts that have been jumping around in her head.

With one push with her legs, Sitheia throw away the covers and jumped out of the bed. Feeling a little embarrassed for having to put on a spare night shirt in the middle of the night as if she was two years old and she has just wet the bed. Dropping the night shirt in a pile on top of her bed, Sitheia started getting ready.

Her outfit consisted of a shirt, pants and a pair of boots. A typical village outfit. Her clothes used to have a yellow creamy kind of color, but with time and use the color has faded almost entirely. Sitheia has been wearing that outfit for three years, and it has been patched many times by now. For years, almost every day she climbed the rocky hill whenever she was going to the tower. With each climb, more holes and patches were added to her clothes.

Eventually Sitheia discovered that she can take a detour around the hill that took her somewhat less than an hour and she can get to the tower without getting scratched and without tearing her clothes. Her mother was very happy when she didn't have to patch any more of her clothes.

One of her most important possessions was her gathering bag that she wore over her shoulder. Spending a lot of time in the woods without gathering some of the useful herbs was just a waste of good opportunity, so she always had her bag over her shoulder. On her belt she also had a tiny little dagger. Even though the dagger was very sharp, it was so small that it was barely as big as the small finger on her hand and it was of no use for anything other than cutting herbs and flowers. Sitheia tried once cutting an apple with it. It was the most work she ever had to do for a single bite.

With the gloves on her hands she looked down at herself and smiled. Her clothes were worn out, true. But, by selling herbs to the herbalist she has saved almost enough money to buy herself a new set of clothes.

Mary Cat, her mother has offered her of course to help her sew a dress, but she had no intention of wearing one. Even less she intended to learn how to sew. She imagined herself climbing on the hill toward the tower with the dress constantly catching on rocks. Picturing herself in a dress on the hill made her feel goosebumps. She almost felt herself falling from the hill because her dress caught on something. Sitheia shivered.

She took a deep breath and exhaled. Now she was ready to face the world. Climbing to the living room Sitheia saw that her family has already finished with breakfast. Her mother and her sister were peeling apples, which made Sitheia smile. She knew what the apples were meant for.

In their family it was something like a tradition, to make a sweet apple pie when someone was having a birthday. Of course, the tradition may have started because of the two apple trees that they had in the backyard. Sitheia liked this tradition, because apple pie was her favorite pie.

"Hey Sitty, we're making a pie." Her little sister saw her first.

"Good morning." Sitheia said to her family.

"Good morning." Her mother said and then added with a worried expression. "Did you get any sleep last night?"

Sitheia did her best to make her smile look sincere.

"Yes, I had no more bad dreams. I am sorry for waking you all up and making you worry." Sitheia said going toward the kitchen table where a plate was waiting for her with fresh bread, a slice of cheese and a cup of milk.

She ate her breakfast in a hurry wanting to get to the temple as soon as possible.

"What are you doing grandpa?" Sitheia said to the old man that was sitting by the fire in his favorite chair. He was rubbing an ointment to his ankles.

"The weather must be changing." Her grandpa said with a wince. "My joints are acting up. Your friend Agnes gave me this ointment. It supposed to lessen the pain, but I doubt it."

"You seem to be in a bit of a rush?" Mary asked seeing that her daughter is throwing the food in her mouth as if she is shoveling snow rushing to finish her breakfast. "Slow down. You'll choke."

"I must be off. I have a lot of things to do today."

Sitheia stopped to catch her breath. "I was planning to go and see acolyte Nigel."

"Of course. This is your last day in class." Her mother noted.

"Yes. But, I want to see him because of the dream that I had last night. I thought that since already I am going to be at the temple, then I can use the opportunity to get refreshed with purification. The thing is that I already planned on going to the woods right after the class so I'll have to do things a lot faster if I am to get everything done before nightfall."

"Why do you need to go to the woods today?" Her sister Dana asked.

"I need to collect some herbs for Mrs. Agnes. Her supplies are dwindling and she always pays well."

"But it's your birthday. You can go tomorrow." Dana said.

The thing was that Sitheia was only looking for an excuse to go to the tower, but that was not something that she was willing to try to explain to her family. The people in the village of Sacred Pools tended to keep their distance from the tower and especially from the Door. But Sitheia didn't believe all that nonsense about the place being cursed.

"Will you be going alone?" Her mother asked before she had the chance to answer her sister.

Sitheia found that question a bit odd.

"That is a strange question. I always go alone." Sitheia said, but then she added. "Actually no, John will be going with me, at least until we get to the Temple. Then, he'll have to work. He is helping the masons."

"You spend a lot of time with that boy." Her mother said.

"Of course I do. He is mine." Sitheia said and her sister giggled.

"What is that supposed to mean?" Her mother frowned. "You are not thinking of getting married to the Last Child, are you?"

Sitheia froze in her steps not believing what her mother just said. Not the marring part, that was nonsense of course. But what she said about John being the Last Child. That was not a polite thing to say.

"Mom! Don't call him like that. It's rude."

"Leave her be, Mary. John is a strong lad. He would be a good husband to her." Her grandpa thought that he was helping her.

"Grandpa! What is wrong with the two of you? I have no intention of getting married." Sitheia said her face red with anger which her mother interpreted as embarrassment.

"Why not? Starting tomorrow you'll be an adult. Creating a family should be one of the things that you will need to do."

"That may be, but not now."

Sitheia couldn't believe where the conversation have gone to. She was young and had her whole life ahead. She was not going to put an end to all her opportunities by getting married as soon as she is old enough. That was madness.

"Then why are you spending so much time with that boy?" Her mother asked continuing to peel the apple.

"As I said, he is mine. I don't have the time to talk right now. Today is going to be a very busy day for me and there are a lot of things that I have to do. Probably I won't be coming back before nightfall. I'll see you tonight."

CHAPTER 3

As Sitheia stepped outside, life pleasantly hit her in the face. The warm sun was a welcoming change to all the cold weather they had to endure for the last almost five months. The warm breeze signaled that spring is coming. Hearing the singing birds from the nearby trees told her that others appreciate the change in the weather as well.

Looking around, she noticed her countrymen rushing to do their daily activities. The farmers were going to work on the fields. The shepherds were taking the sheep herds to the pastures. Song came from the river bands where the fishermen threw their nets. She could smell the freshly baked bread coming from the bakery. She could hear the hammering of the blacksmith coming from the house behind theirs. The whole Sacred Pools was simply bursting with life.

Suddenly Sitheia felt a gush of wind. Looking up she spotted the most amazing creature that she has ever seen. It looked just like a horse only it had wings. The Pegasus was flying high above the roofs, but it managed to stir the already vibrant village. The people, both the young and the old cheered together the celestial being. This was a great way to start the day.

Turning to the right, she saw a large man with boyish face awkwardly sitting at the stairs in front of the neighboring house. That was John. He was seven years older. He was six feet tall. He had broad shoulders and had very short dark blond hair with blue eyes. Whenever Sitheia spoke of John, she would say that he belongs to her. In a manner, he did.

When she first met John, he was broken. Her mother earlier called him the Last child. Sitheia hated that nickname. It was the name that the Cat people used to sort of mark him, because he was the last child that was born before the seven years long drought that fell on her people.

For seven years not a single child was born in all the Cat villages and the superstitious folk believed that it was because the last child being born was unlucky. When someone was using the Last child nickname, it was like they were cursing him for being born. And that just made her blood boil with anger at the injustice.

And then Sitheia came to this world and the drought ended. For his entire life John did everything he could to prove that he has worth and value to give. He worked hard and helped everyone whenever he could, but it was never enough.

The villagers believed that he was cursed or at least that he was unlucky and they preferred to avoid him completely disregarding his good intentions. Even his family most of the time pretended as if he does not exist.

When Sitheia met him and learn about his fate, she became furious. Unlike the rest of the Cat who preferred to accept things in life as they were as long as they were in line with their beliefs, Sitheia did not accepted anything that she didn't like or approved. As a Cat person, John needed to belong, to be a part of something. So, when Sitheia said to him:

"I will take care of you. From now on, you are mine." Sitheia said feeling like the words were not coming from her, but from some hidden part inside her soul that lay buried under the surface. "You will do as I say and no one will ever hurt you again. Do you accept?" Saying those words felt strange to her, but it also felt right and she had no regrets or hidden agendas.

John accepted without hesitation. He bowed his head to her and then he hugged her and stayed in her embrace for a long time. She felt that they have established a very special kind of connection that day that remained strong ever since.

John was big and strong and he was more than capable of taking care of himself. But, the scars that his family and the rest of the Cat have left on his soul have made his willpower so small that he had no desire to live on his own.

Sitheia helped him with that. She forced him to believe that he has value and that he is needed in the world. Sitheia encouraged him to take care of himself and to not let people push him around. She opened his eyes and made him love and appreciates life. Even though John pretended that he was a little dumb in front of other people, so they would leave him alone, Sitheia knew that he was actually very intelligent. When they would start talking, he had no problem keeping his end of the conversation.

Sitheia stretched her arms in a non-lady like fashion, basking in the sunlight and then she went to say hello to John who still had his eyes on the sky. A Pegasus was not a common thing to see for anyone in the village.

"Did you see that?" She said stopping in front of him. As soon as John saw her, his face lit up and he jumped on his feet.

"Hey, Sitty. Yea, I saw it, a Pegasus. If someone had ever told me that I will see one flying over our homes I would have never believed it."

"I know what you mean. For some reason they all seem to be avoiding this place." She said.

"I wonder where he was going."

Every time she stood in front of John, she was amazed at how tall he was. He had broad shoulders and you could say that he was handsome. Not Lords of Perdival kind of handsome, but still he was pleasant to look at.

"Probably he is going home, to a nest on top of a mountain where the other flying horses sleep." Sitheia said childishly.

"I don't really think that horses live in nests, not even flying ones." John noted with a small smile.

"Really? I always thought that they were just like birds." Sitheia said with a smile that made John wonder if she was serious or not.

"Actually, they are more like regular horses. They just have wings." John explained as they started walking. "So, are you ready for your last day in school?" He teased.

Sitheia looked at him sideways checking if he was serious. Seeing that he wasn't serious made her smile. She thought that going for her last class was a waste of time, but it was part of their tradition. And the Cat loved their traditions.

"We'll see. Come, we need to be going." She said looking back over her shoulder.

"What? What's wrong?" He asked noticing her

edginess.

"It's nothing. I just feel kind of exposed walking in the middle of the street." She said looking left and right.

"You do know that you are being weird, right?"

"Thanks."

"I mean weirder than usual. What is going on?" He repeated his question.

Sitheia stopped walking and turned to face him. Making sure that there was no one around them she leaned in and whispered.

"I had a bad dream last night." She whispered making sure no one overhears them. "That is the other reason why I am going to the temple."

"You want to go through a purification ritual?" John asked her a little worried as they started moving again.

"I do."

"Again?"

"What that's supposed to mean?" She said throwing him a nasty look.

"Nothing." He raised his hands in 'I surrender' sort of way. "I'm just saying that you are visiting that temple a little too often. I am not sure if it's healthy to go through purification as often as you are."

Sitheia stopped walking and turned to face him.

"Look, I don't like it either. But, these rituals are helping me. They really are."

John studied her face for a moment.

"It's not just a bad dream, is it?"

Sitheia didn't respond. She just turned and started walking slowly, wishing that one day people can just sprout wings on their backs just like the Pegasus and fly to where they need to get without the fuss of meeting people along the way.

"You had another episode, have you?" John asked following her closely. He took her silence as a 'Yes'. "Goddess." He whispered.

"That is new. When did they put up that food stand over there?" Sitheia pointed toward a stand filled with various types of fresh veggies. John gave her a questioning look. "What?"

"When Nick and Ellie got married, they moved in together. They set up that stand to sell the veggies from their farm. That was almost nine months ago." John said.

"Oh." Sitheia said suspecting that John was wondering on what world she has been living for the past nine months. "Well, I tend to avoid walking out in the open. I prefer to move through the shadows. That way I stay away from other people's business and they have no choice but to stay away from mine."

"Sounds like a good strategy." John said in a neutral way.

"It is. I am tired of everyone butting in on everything

that I am doing and judging me on every decision I make."

Moving next to her, John was having no problem measuring his steps to match hers.

"So, what was it about?" He asked making her turn to look at his face.

John was reliable. Telling him about her dream was not a bad idea. He was smart enough to be able to help her figure out what is the meaning of the dream. And also there was no chance that he would ever betray her trust and say something about it to anyone.

It was just that even though she was ignoring everyone that they passed without difficulty, there were still too many people on the street that could overhear them. In a small place like Sacred Pools, there were no secrets, unless you actively avoid everyone so that no one can get close enough so they can learn your secrets. That last part was Sitheia's default plan for everything that was her business and concerned nobody else.

"I'll tell you later. There are too many ears on the road."

There was no need to explain what she meant. Sitheia couldn't understand how her countrymen were so stupid and were unable to see the huge potential that was in John. Sitheia liked to have a positive outlook on life. When Sitheia would look at something, she never saw what was but what it could become.

Unlike her, the rest of the Cat were not that forward

thinking people. While they were usually friendly and generous, they were also very serious about maintaining their way of life. If they believed that something or someone was not approved by the Goddess or the Lords of Perdival, than they took it as a threat. They didn't need proof or evidence whether that was true or not. Having her own people behave in such "idiotic" way was breaking her heart. For a kind and peaceful folk like the Cat, being judgmental about anything or anyone was just silly.

They were still very far when they spotted the black hole in the mountain on the other side of the village. The entrance to the temple was so big that it wasn't difficult to see it from a great distance.

"They could have placed the temple in the middle of Sacred Pools." John wiped the sweat from his brow.

"You are not getting tired, are you John?" Sitheia teased.

"Who? Me? No. It's just getting hot." He said with a smile.

"Come on, we can really use a bit of a sunlight after that freezing cold weather we had. I swear it. That was the coldest winter that I can remember." Sitheia enjoyed the sun, basking in the warmth with half closed eyes.

"You're saying that every year."

"That's because it's true. Look." Sitheia pointed far ahead of them toward a wide bridge that looked to be halfway between them and the temple's entrance. "There's the bridge, we are almost there."

After crossing the bridge at the edge of the village, the entrance to the temple was no longer just a dark hole on the side of the mountain. From down here Sitheia was only able to see the top end of the entrance that went in an arc, but she knew that the closer they get, the bigger it will turn out to be. Every time she went to the temple, Sitheia was amazed by the size of it. To her it looked like it was impossible to build something of that magnitude.

Before starting on the path that leads to the temple Sitheia looked toward the one that lead northwest toward the sea and to the small island where their masters lived. Even though she has never taken that road, it always made her feel curious and eager to see where it leads.

The road to the sea had some curves, but at least it was leveled. The path that leads to the temple was steppe and it involved a little bit of climbing.

As they both started on the steppe path, Sitheia looked sideways toward John.

"I told you why I am going to the temple." She said. "What is your reason for going to the temple?"

"There have been some cracks appearing in some stairway. Acolyte Thomas has asked the masons to fix it before an accident happens. I'm going there to help the masons." John said it with a smile, but he wasn't able to hide the clenched jaw from Sitheia.

Whenever someone needed help in the village, John was there to help. No one ever thanked him or even acknowledged his presence. That injustice made her heart burn with anger.

"Wow. You are so angry right now that actual smoke is coming out of your ears." John teased her.

She didn't smile at his joke. With everything that has happened and was still happening to him, he was still trying to be positive and to look like everything was perfect. That made her even angrier.

"Why are you angry?" He said with his smile fading. "Are you angry at me?"

That question made some of her fury to dissipate.

"I am not angry at you, John. I can never be angry at you." Sitheia said happy that the smile returned to his face. "I am angry with how good and helpful you are without even a 'thank you' in return. I am angry at the people that are taking advantage of your goodness. You think that I don't know that they have called you to help, but they intend on letting you do all the hard work? Bah, I am so furious that I want to go punch those 'masons' in their stupid faces."

"I'd love to see that." John said with a small smile, but then he lowered his eyes. "What choice do I have? I am who I am and there is nothing that I can do about it.

I just have to accept that people will never be OK with my birth and I'll have to learn to live with it. It's just hard sometimes."

"If they can't accept you, then it's their loss. You need to stop seeking their approval. John, you are a great guy and you don't need them. You need to believe in yourself as much I believe in you and I am sure that you will achieve great things in life. I believe in you."

They were looking in each other's eyes for a while after Sitheia stopped talking. Eventually, the sadness disappeared from John's eyes and the burning anger quieted down in Sitheia.

"Are you going to be OK?" She asked. John nodded as a response. "I'm glad. Come on, break's over. Let's move on."

His lips spread into a smile as he followed Sitheia up the path.

The temple was a magnificent structure unlike any that Sitheia has ever seen. You can see the entrance from a far if you are actually looking for it. But, somehow on the way up, there are so many things that are drawing your attention. Distracted by the view, by the steppe path and by the other pilgrims that are walking the same road, it was easy to lose sight of your goal. Somehow, the sixteen feet tall entrance sneaks up on you and you fail to notice it until you are right in front of it.

Whenever Sitheia would be visiting the temple, on many occasions she would question her eyes if they were working properly. It was unnerving how she always failed to notice the decorations until she got within three feet distance from them.

It was also weird that on each visit the decorations looked to be different. Once she would see the image of a dragon, but the next time instead of dragon, there was a fish. Many times the stone tablets were empty without any decorations and sometimes they just seemed to be blurred. As if her eyes were unable to focus on them at all.

The wind was blowing strong in here. It was strong enough that with the help of the dirt and the dust, the wind was visibly obscuring the temple from sight.

The steps leading to the entrance were not big but they were many and together they formed a steppe path that was difficult to climb. The steps weren't tall, but their number was so great that it was taxing to walk them.

When at last they got to the top and there were no more steps left to climb, they were breathing heavily. On a cue from Sitheia they both stopped for a moment to take a breath and slow down their breathing before they go into the temple.

It was only after they rested for a while that they took in the giant structure from which only the entrance was visible.

"That is enormous." Sitheia said for like a hundredth time.

Despite that she has seen the entrance so many times before, it never ceased to amaze her. From the outside, the temple was a magnificent structure with all sorts of weird decorations that Sitheia couldn't understand what they were supposed to mean. But, Sitheia knew that the parts that were visible from the outside were only for show. The real temple was entirely underground and considering that inside lived and worked hundreds of people, she suspected that it went on under the entire mountain.

Noticing that John was not following her, Sitheia turned to look at her companion. He was bent over the road looking at something. When she joined him trying to find out at what he was looking at, he waved her over pointing toward the road.

"You see how these steps are a little different than the background?" He asked.

Sitheia had no idea why or what she was looking at the road but she humored him.

"Yes, the steps don't have the same color. What about them?"

"Not all the steps have different color." John said pointing at several steps. "Every fourth step is the same color as the base."

"So?" Sitheia was still not certain what was interesting

about steps with different colors.

"I've heard stories from the masons that I've been working with. These steps with light gray color have been added long after the temple was built. Before that, only the one with dark gray color existed."

"So, what are you saying?" Sitheia asked.

"I am saying that when the temple was built, it wasn't meant to be used by Cat people."

"Then by who?"

"I have no idea. But look at this huge entrance. It doesn't look like it was made for anyone that I know." John said with a smile.

"Maybe it was made this big so that it would be easier for them to bring furniture inside." She suggested.

"Seriously?"

"Yea, I've heard what I just said." Sitheia admitted. "But, I didn't get much sleep last night, so I'm getting a pass."

"Fine." He said and she could tell that he was making an effort not to start laughing out loud. Looking at his face she noticed that it was much brighter than when they were walking through the village. 'He really finds these things interesting.' She thought feeling good that at least some parts of his soul were safe and happy.

CHAPTER 4

Once they were inside the antechamber, John went looking for acolyte Thomas leaving Sitheia alone in the spacious entry chamber. The smell of burning candles and incense was strong inside and it took her some time to adjust her breathing to the temple's strange air.

There were many doors both on the left and the right side of the antechamber, but because of the size of the room they all looked miniscule. The walls on either side were half natural half built. It wasn't difficult to spot where the masons have practiced their craft, but it was obvious that the base of the walls was the mountain itself.

Murals were painted everywhere. There were many smaller murals on the floor. Most of them with images of the stars, and there were also several larger murals on the walls. Sitheia noticed that there were many symbols that represented the power of the sun and they were all over the floor. Sitheia also noticed that in some places the sun was burning bright and in others it had only a faint glow.

What always picked her curiosity were the larger murals on the walls. They were images of a huge three headed dragon whose heads were all in different colors. Sitheia could never understand what that dragon was doing in what was supposed to be home to their Goddess.

Sitheia stopped herself right there. It wasn't really their Goddess. Long time ago, around the time when the bargain was made, the Cat have adopted the religion and beliefs of their masters. If they ever had different gods or beliefs before, there was no record left. But it didn't really matter. The Goddess, just like the Lords of Perdival looked after them and took care of them. That was enough for the Goddess to earn the fate of her people.

In the lives of the Cat people, the temple played a great role and it was not just a religious one. The part of the temple that was actually a temple, was the part that the Cat actively avoided unless they were desperate.

The other part of the temple was dedicated for the education the young Cat until they come of age. For the bigger part of her life, few hours every week Sitheia have spent learning all that is necessary for a Cat to survive.

She studied things like how to read and write and things concerning the bargain. After all, it was because of the bargain with the Lords of Perdival that the Cat managed to stay alive.

Of course, in all the history lessons she got at the temple, there was never mentioning of any battles. So Sitheia didn't find them to be very interesting. At least not as interesting as those stories that she got from her grandfather. Thankfully, after today she will never have to hear another lesson, which is why she needed to find acolyte Nigel as soon as possible and get this over with.

Because she has been walking the corridors of the educational area of the temple for so long, Sitheia had no difficulty navigating to the classroom where acolyte Nigel was teaching.

Everyone else was already here and in their seats and acolyte Nigel was standing behind a small worn out desk with several scrolls in front of him.

The rest of the class was consisted of young adults that were several years younger than she was. That was another reason why she didn't like school. All the other kids were the same age with each other, but because of her First Child status there was no one at her age.

That is why she had to take classes with kids that were younger than she was. Naturally, the other kids kept to their own age. They respected her, she couldn't deny that. But, sometimes she wanted friendship more than she wanted respect.

Sitheia smiled looking at her classmates. Whatever issues she might have had because of her growing up without any real friends were now gone. She had a friend now, a very special friend that she intended to visit after she was done with the temple.

"Ah, Sitty. You are here." Acolyte Nigel smiled at her and pointed toward her seat. "Take your seat and we can begin."

Sitheia took her seat and was getting ready to tune out, but something made her to stop. For some reason, acolyte Nigel was watching her. She was careful to keep her mind clear of any thoughts, because it was not a secret that all the acolytes were able to read minds to a certain point.

"Since today is the last lesson for one of you, I would like for us to go over some basic necessities. Tips, if that's how you would prefer to call them. These are vital tips that your survival may depend upon them.

Cooking, hunting, farming, mining, making tools, building houses, knitting, and sewing are skills that we use every day. These skills are very important for maintaining our way of life. Some of you have learned some of these skills and in time you will master them, while others have shown affinity for other skills.

If you put in time and hard work, you can learn some

and even all of them if that is what you want. Only, the problem with trying to learn all of them is that it will take you so much time that you won't get to use all of them while you live.

Or, you can at least learn the ones that you are going to choose as your professions. Those are skills that you will be using for most of your life.

But, there are certain things that our people can never learn. We are a peaceful folk. Not just that we are not good at making war, we are the exact opposite of it. We thrive on kindness and generosity. Unfortunately, there are many powerful forces out there that whish ill to our people. We have inherited plenty of enemies that wait for us outside the safe territory that belongs to the Lords of Perdival.

The bargain that our ancestors struck with the original Lord Perdival is our most sacred heritage. The heart of the Cat is in that bargain. Without it, we would have been extinct thousands of years ago.

As long as we all maintain the conditions of the bargain, we are safe. We serve and they protect. It's that simple.

With the Cat being hidden from the world for so long, most of the demons that once hunted our ancestors have gone dormant. But, there are few left possessing people on very high and influential positions. They are always on the lookout for any sign of our existence and for the chance to vanquish us for good. One such possession that we are aware of is High King Memnon."

Acolyte Nigel had to stop because his last sentence was followed by a lot of rumbling and murmuring among his students.

"We have suspicions that there are few others in this country, but we have no confirmation. Sitty…" He said and everyone's eyes focused on her. "Starting tomorrow, you will be an adult. Of course, you will pick profession that will help you contribute to our society and maybe one day you will be chosen to go and work at the castle.

To be chosen is a great honor for any Cat. But, if that happens and for some reason you have to leave our protected land, bear in mind what I have just told you. The demons are still out there. They are hidden just like we are. They are waiting for someone, perhaps you to reveal yourself to them so they can use you to devour us all.

As my final lesson for you Sitty, and this you all need to remember. Never forget. We depend on the bargain. As long as both sides keep their end of the bargain we are safe. This is why we must keep it safe at all costs."

That lecturing did not make Sitheia feel any better and she was relieved when they were dismissed at last and she was allowed to get out of there.

It was a relief to be back in the antechamber. That lecture about demons hiding amongst the people and one of them being the High King, it scared her pretty bad. Combining it with the dream that she had last night and she was properly freaked out. Sitheia could feel her back getting cold with sweat. She had to find Katherine and do the ritual. Demons. Is that what the monsters from her dream were? She didn't want to know. All she wanted was to forget about the whole thing and stop having scary dreams.

Sitheia wasn't sure where to look for the acolyte Katherine. She remembered through what door Katherine usually took her, but she also knew that she was not allowed to go wandering through the temple on her own without someone to keep an eye on her. Not sure what to do, Sitheia decided to look inside the Hall of Prayers planning to ask some of the priests about acolyte Katherine.

The Hall of Prayers was an eerie place. It was a relatively large semicircular hall. The ceilings were so high that they couldn't be seen at all. It may have something to do with the poor light of the hall, but looking up was like looking into darkness.

At the far end of the hall there was a shrine with a large brazier that the priests used for offering sacrifices. Behind the brazier there was an enormous mural covering the wall. The entire mural was one image of the same three headed dragon blowing fire from each head. Facing the shrine there were many rows of benches where the worshipers can sit or kneel and prey. Spread out through the hall there were many candelabras illuminating the place.

There were only several villagers praying at the moment, but there was no one from the temple that she could ask for the whereabouts of acolyte Katherine. There was one priestess in dark red robes kneeling in front of the shrine, but she knew that that type of priests never talked.

Sitheia decided to wait here for a while and sat on an empty bench at the front so that she would not disturb the others. There was something about this place that just made her be quiet and careful not to disturb the general peacefulness of the place. Like any noise made might be considered a grievous offense.

Looking up front at the shrine her eyes fell on a bust that was the only representation of the Goddess that was in human form rather than as a dragon. The bust was milky white and it made Sitheia feel strange looking at it. It felt so real like it was alive and it was looking back at her.

Pulling her eyes from the bust, Sitheia considered praying. She never had much luck with praying. It felt weird to her trying to speak to the Goddess in any way. She was happy with her life and didn't want to ask for anything. If she was supposed to talk to the Goddess and confess her secrets, than Sitheia already had someone for that.

Lifting her head, Sitheia tried to relax by looking at the beautiful star that was engraved in the center of a big circular shield that was positioned just a little above the bust. Every time that she would come here, looking at that star made her calm down.

Her eye moved across the mural of the three headed dragon and she felt annoyed. She was starting to get irritated with all the images of her people's Goddess in the form of a dragon.

'Why on earth are we worshiping a three headed dragon?' Sitheia thought before she could stop herself.

The figure at the shrine for which Sitheia assumed was a priestess lifted her head. Sitheia instinctively put her hand over her mouth even though it was not her mouth that was putting her in trouble. She should have remembered that nearly all of the priests were capable of reading minds. Fortunately, most of the priests choose not to waste their voice by talking with regular people, especially about mundane topics such as unruly thoughts of a soon to be adult. The priestess returned her head in the bowed position making Sitheia let go of her breath for which she wasn't aware that she was holding.

"It is rude to interrupt a priestess during her prayer." A female voice coming from behind made Sitheia jump and squeal.

Turning, Sitheia saw that behind her was a female acolyte. She was older than her and at least a full head taller. This was Katherine, the acolyte that usually performed her purification. Sitheia liked her. The tall acolyte always had an interesting sense of humor.

"Wow thank you, Sitty. I have always liked you too." The acolyte responded to her thoughts.

"Hey…" Sitheia started. 'What was her name? I always seemed to forget. Crap. She'll read that too.'

"Really? Really, Sitty? After all the times that I have removed from your head all the nasty things that you have a habit of picking up, and you don't even remember my name?" The acolyte pretended to get angry and then she suddenly stopped, seeing that Sitheia was smirking. "Oh. You're good. You're really good."

"I got you." Sitheia laughed. "Hello, Katherine. How are you today?"

"Better now, that someone with actual brains has come in. Cat are the most good-natured people in the world, I'll give you that. But I can't believe how boring it is to be around them." Katherine complained.

"Really?" Sitheia asked with a smile.

"If there was a way for me to read the mind of a sparrow, I am sure that it would have more interesting thoughts than a Cat. But, that doesn't apply to you. You are different. So, how may this humble acolyte be of service to you today? Have you come to cleanse your sins?"

"I have no sins that need cleansing, but purifying my spirit and the ache in my limbs would be nice."

"Oh, you have sins, sweetheart. I am sure of that. For

some reason I can't see them in your mind, but I know that they are there. I can feel them underneath the surface, but somehow you are hiding them." Katherine said stepping forward invading Sitheia's personal space. She was looking in her eyes as if she was trying to peek through a window into Sitheia's soul.

"Aren't you supposed to be trying to help me, instead of poking through my mind,?" Sitheia responded defiantly looking back in the acolyte's eyes.

"Of course I am here to help you, honey. But, I am allowed to have some fun while I am doing it. As I said, I am bored." Katherine smiled leaning closer. "So, little dove. What is troubling you?"

"I've had a bad dream last night." Sitheia said not backing off.

"Don't tell me, let me guess. Was it about giant spiders, or about a two headed bear? I know, it was about a giant mushroom with bulging eyes." Katherine's eyes opened wide as she was guessing teasingly.

"I am serious." Sitheia rolled her eyes.

"Oh, pumpkin, so am I. So what was it about? Has old Uncle Peter been telling you stories, again? Have you been wetting your bed?" The acolyte whispered leaning so close that Sitheia could feel her warm breath on her face. It had the scent of vanilla and cinnamon.

"Katherine, as cute as you are, I got to admit that you

are totally mad." Sitheia said thinking 'Damn, her breath is intoxicating.'

"Oh, lollipop. You are so sweat. I like you too, but I am afraid that I am kind of taken. Vows and all. Belong to the Goddess for life. That kind of things, you know." Katherine giggled playfully. "But, we are disturbing High priestess Melinda in her prayers. If you want to talk about your dream dear, we will have to do it while we walk toward the preparation chamber." Katherine backed away a bit.

"Sure." Sitheia was eager to get everything finished as soon as possible.

"Sitty, don't rush me, princess. We'll finish when we finish." Katherine said making Sitheia roll her eyes again.

The acolyte took Sitheia's hand and led her toward a door to the left. Before they got out of the Hall of Prayers, Katherine stopped suddenly and turned toward Sitheia.

"The High priestess wants me to give you a message. The three headed dragon is only a spiritual manifestation of our Goddess, not her physical form. Each head represents a different aspect of her power. The blue head is the healer, the black head is the killer and the red head is the balance between them."

Once they left the Hall of Prayers with Katherine in the lead, Sitheia recognized the path that she has walked so many times before.

"Sitty? Why the High priestess gave you that message?"

Katherine asked with a confused expression. Sitheia made a sour face before answering.

"Because I forgot where I was for a moment and I couldn't keep my mental mouth shut." She said irritably making Katherine giggle.

"Mental mouth, hahaha. I like that." Katherine laughed. "So tell me, what did you dream about?"

Sitheia wasn't certain how much she should reveal, but she did come to the temple looking for some help with her dream. She told acolyte Katherine about her 'episode'.

Sitheia mentioned every detail about it that she could remember with one slight change. She didn't mention the tower at all. Instead, she said that she couldn't recognize the place.

She was amazed that Katherine was listening to her carefully without interrupting or making any inappropriate comments.

"What do you think?" Sitheia asked once she finished retelling her dream.

"You haven't had one of these 'episodes' in a very long time." Katherine said with a serious expression. "Why now?"

"I thought that you were going to tell me the answer to that question." Sitheia responded with concern in her voice. "Most importantly, I need to know, what I have to do to avoid this happening again."

"I would very much love to tell you that you need to do this or do that and it will all go away. But, I can't." Katherine said with compassion in her eyes. "The only thing that I believe that may help you is the very thing that you are doing right now. The ritual of purification should remove any afflictions that you may have."

"Should? That is not very comforting."

"I don't want to lie to you, little dove. Perhaps, this is not a bad thing. Maybe it is a message from the Goddess." The acolyte said. Katherine made another turn and they have reached the preparation chamber.

Sitheia was not very happy with the thing that she heard from the acolyte, but maybe Katherine was right. Not about the dream being a message from the Goddess, but that after the ritual it will all go away.

From the entire temple, the Preparation chamber was the least favorite part for Sitheia. She thought that it was totally unnecessary.

Katherine and some other acolytes have told her for like thousandth times. Before anyone in need of purification was allowed in the sacred pools, they needed first to have their body prepared for the heavily enchanted water.

If anyone tried to go into the pools without first having their body prepared, they risked going insane or they even might drop dead before they manage to get out of the water. Sitheia hated the preparation because it always made her feel sick.

"Come on, it's not that bad. Besides, if you are to get better, first you need to get a little sick. Everybody knows that."

Sitheia choose not to respond, whether by using her voice or by thinking the answers. For one thing, in the Preparation chamber was forbidden for anyone to speak. This was a place where the first part of the ritual of cleansing took place and the acolytes or priests needed to concentrate without any distractions, although priests participated in this part of the ceremony on very rear occasions.

Katherine led her forward down a long hallway that had many doors left and right. She finally stopped walking and Sitheia could swear that she saw her ears moving.

'Here. This one is unoccupied and ready for use.' The acolyte sent her thoughts toward Sitheia leading her to a smaller room to the right.

The room was small and empty of any furniture except for one candelabrum in the corner. On one side there was a bed made of stone that was sticking out of the wall. Next to the bed there was a stone basin filled with water from the pools that was so pure and clean that you could easily see the bottom of the basin event though it was a little deep. The only other thing in the room was a little cabinet from which Katherine pulled a small wooden box.

"You know the drill Sitty." Katherine pointed toward

the bed.

Sitheia did know the drill, but despite wanting to stall as much as possible, she still had a long list of things that she needed to do today. Without any more delays, Sitheia walked toward the bed and she started removing her clothes. One after the other she dropped all of her clothes in a pile next to the bed.

When she was done, Katherine have already prepared something like a thin nightshirt and handed it over to Sitheia who pulled it on right away. Replacing her clothes with that nightshirt was probably the only thing that Sitheia didn't mind from the preparations. The main part of the ritual was being dipped into the water from the sacred pools and if she was wearing her own clothes she would need hours in front of a fire in order to dry off her clothes. Though, she should wash her clothes, eventually.

'Are you ready? Come, drink up and let's get to work.' She heard Katherine's thoughts flowing through her mind. She looked down in front of her. Katherine was holding a small vial with golden liquid in it, that she was offering to her.

Sitheia reached out for the vial, but she hesitated to drink it. Sitheia was grateful that the acolyte was not rushing her to hurry up, and she was also not intruding her mind even though she was aware that Katherine was following every thought that came to her. She knew that for the ritual to be successful, it needed to be done by her own will. It couldn't be forced or hurried. It had to take its natural course. Katherine was very patient, but Sitheia knew that stalling was pointless and an unnecessary waste of time.

Sitheia looked at the vial again. She knew very well what that vial was capable of making her feel. The memory was crystal clear of previous occasions when she was being offered a vial just like this one and the pain that followed afterward. It was a feeling worse than any sickness or injury she has ever experienced. It was like taking poison by her own free will with the belief that it was going to make her feel better afterwards.

It was silly, she knew that. Each time she was about to take that potion she feared that it will be her last time, that she will become a mindless statue and she will never break out of the trance. Sitheia also knew that the potion never worked on her the way it was meant to work.

Sitheia uncorked the vial, raised it toward the waiting acolyte as in a toast and emptied the bottle.

The world instantly stopped being so solid and started to resemble more like a place filled with purple fog. Sitheia was certain that the potion was supposed to dull the mind, not just lower the inhibitions in a person. Then why her mind was working so much faster. At least that is what she thought.

Her eyes darted all around the room. Were they underground? How is it that there were basins filled with so much water when they were already underground? She could hear water running nearby. Something nice and soft brushed her forehead. It was wet. Sitheia tried to focus her eyes, but her vision was all blurry. On moments when she was able to open her eyes she saw Katherine dipping a sponge in the basin filled and then she would brush the skin on her forehead with it.

Her nostrils flared at the scent of cinnamon and vanilla. Katherine was close. It was all right.

Then the pain hit her in her guts making her double over. She felt a sharp pain like a knife piercing her body. The pain started appearing in each of her organs one after the other. She thought that her heart was going to explode until she could no longer breathe.

Maybe it lasted a minute or an hour, Sitheia couldn't say. But, when she came back to her senses, she was lying on the stone bad with Katherine sitting next to her and brushing her forehead.

'Welcome back.' Sitheia felt Katherine's mind speaking in her head. 'Are you ok?'

Sitheia nodded still very shaken up and unable to form a coherent thought.

'We are done with this part.' The acolyte thought. 'Do you need to rest or we can proceed with the second part?'

'I'm ok. I can do this.' Sitheia thought and tried to get up, but the acolyte put a hand on her chest to keep her still.

'Not yet. Here, drink this.' Katherine offered her a second vial. This one with liquid that had pink color that even in this light was distinguishable.

Sitheia remembered this vial as well. The first potion brought pain, while the second was supposed to dull the mind. To lower the natural defenses so that the body does not try to resist the powers of the water.

Sitheia took the vial and drank it at once. The world slowed down and lost focus. Looking at her own arm, Sitheia could see her fingers moving in a blur. She could hear nothing around her but a dripping sound like water falling drop by drop.

Sitheia realized that she was no longer lying on the stone bed. She was walking and there was a hand on her back between her shoulder blades. Sitheia saw shadows moving in front of her.

'Don't be afraid. You are safe.' Sitheia heard inside her mind. Whose voice was that and why was it so close to her? Memory of the acolyte Katherine appeared in her mind.

'Stop fighting the potion or you'll wake up.' That was Katherine again speaking to her mind. Fighting? She wasn't fighting anything. To wake up... that sounded like a good idea.

Her mind felt so light, free of all worries and

inhibitions. It was so peaceful and relaxing. Then why she felt so vulnerable and without any control. Sitheia liked having control over herself and her actions.

'Stop that. You are pushing back against the potion too hard. You should be in a trance.' Katherine thought.

'The cleansing goes deeper if the person is in a state of trance and it is easier on the mind.' Katherine continued.

'You woke up to soon. You are not in a trance.'

With every message that Sitheia received from Katherine, her mind worked clearer and clearer. Like every time before. The potion always failed to keep her in the trance.

'It may not work for you properly. It may hurt you instead.'

'It will work. I have never been in a trance during the last part.' Sitheia responded to the acolyte with her mind.

'I know.' Katherine thought. 'For some reason, you are different. Why is that?'

'I don't know.' Sitheia thought and an image of the Door flashed through her mind. Oh no, she could not have seen that. Her relationship with the Door was her secret. She didn't want others to know about it.

'I haven't seen what?' Katherine asked moving closer and for the millionth time today she invaded Sitheia's personal space. Without any more thoughts, Katherine pulled back and continued to lead.

Exiting from the long hallway, Katherine took her hand and guided her through a narrow tunnel that felt more like the inside of a cave, than a corridor inside a temple. While they were walking, Sitheia heard Katherine chanting words that she couldn't understand. After what seemed like hours of walking through a maze of tunnels they stopped. On the side of the tunnel there was an opening like a doorway and Katherine took her through.

The place where the acolyte took her was very dark. It was illuminated only by the glow of the two torches on either side of the entrance. Sitheia could not see the ceiling, but she could hear water falling down like a waterfall. Walking down the stone steps, Katherine took her down to where the dark pool was beginning. The water looked so dark because there was so little light in here, but Sitheia knew that it was not very deep. There were walls inside the pool that separated the segment where Sitheia was, from the rest of the underground lake.

The acolyte led her into the water constantly chanting. When they were all in the water to their waist, Katherine put a hand over her head and pushed her under the surface. She did this seven times before she let her rest.

"Come out when you are done, I'll be waiting for you outside." Katherine said and she climbed out into the tunnel.

Sitheia was grateful that she was finally alone. She has

never been comfortable with the preparation part of the ritual. She thought that maybe she was never comfortable because the potion never fully worked on her as it did with the others. When she was younger, she managed to slip in one of the other preparation rooms where a middle aged woman was being prepared for the ritual. Sitheia remembered the empty look on her the woman's face, like there was no one inside. She shuddered at the memory. She wanted never to be as mindless and helpless as that woman was.

She has complained to her mother once after one of her 'episodes' that she didn't want to get cleansed because the potion that the acolytes gave her was making her sick. Her mother laughed. She said that if the body is to become better, then it has to get sick first. It was the same thing that Katherine said to her earlier.

Sitheia didn't agree with the getting sick part, but she had to admit that it was working. All the exhaustion that was in her muscles, all the tension that she felt in her mind, all of it was gone. She was at full strength again. She would have preferred to stay swimming in the dark water forever, but she knew that it was time to get this over with and continue with her plans for the day.

CHAPTER 5

After exiting the enchanted water, Katherine guided Sitheia back to the Preparation room so she can recover her possessions. Despite being energized by the healing powers of the Sacred Pools, Sitheia felt even better once she was back in her own clothes. Still feeling a little dizzy, Sitheia needed to sit down for a moment to get her head right.

"So sweetroll, are you feeling better now?" Katherine said while measuring Sitheia from head to toe with her eyes.

"I do, thank you." Sitheia said leaning back on the wall. "That water is amazing. Tell me, how does one little dip in the pool can make everything better?"

"It's Divine magic, sugar."

"No, seriously. How does it work?"

"Duckling, are you asking me to reveal to you the secrets of our temple? The secret to our Divine healing?"

"Yes. Tell me." Sitheia responded looking Katherine in the eyes. "What is the secret?"

"You should know the answer already. Every Cat should." Katherine smirked.

"All I know is that the sacred pool is blessed by the Goddess, but I don't understand how that works."

"For every other Cat, that would be a sufficient answer. Why are you different?" Katherine invaded Sitheia's personal space again, fixating her with her eyes.

"Are you trying to read my mind? Are you trying to learn my secrets?" Sitheia asked breathing unsteadily.

"I am and I am failing. Why?"

"Are you trying to spell me?"

"Yes, you should obey me and answer me truthfully."

An image of the Door flashed through Sitheia's mind and she immediately knew what she was supposed to do. She stepped forward into Katherine's personal space and got her eyes so close to the eyes of the acolyte that they were breathing in each other's mouths.

"Tell me. How does the healing work?" Sitheia whispered making Katherine to shiver. She saw the eyes of the acolyte open wide and her pupils dilate like a window to her soul that has been open.

"Every priest at the temple adds their blessing to

the sacred pool twice a day to empower it." Katherine explained. "During the Preparation part of the ritual, we numb the body and the mind with the potion. That helps us prepare the body to make it more acceptable for the blessings. The Cat that is receiving the treatment must be totally relaxed. Otherwise the enchantments of the healing water won't be able to penetrate the natural barrier that the human spirit creates around the body."

"So, it's all just your own healing power. I thought that you were praying to the Goddess and she responded by granting the healing." Sitheia said sounding a little disappointed.

"From where do you think that our powers are coming? Without the preparation, the water may kill the person. If the Goddess does not want you to be healed, our powers wouldn't work. If the Goddess wills it, you may drop dead even with the preparation. That is Divine magic. It comes from the Goddess." Katherine finished and Sitheia pulled back a little.

Katherine shocked her head as if waking from a trance. She looked at Sitheia with wide eyes and an expression that Sitheia has never seen on her face before. Fear.

"What did you do to me?"

Before Sitheia could understand what Katherine was asking her, something attracted their attention. At the other end of the corridor a priest stood facing them. Sitheia did not recognized him, but she didn't like the way that he was looking at them, more specifically how he looked at Katherine. Like all other priests he was dressed in dark red robes. His cowl was pulled back and Sitheia could see that he had hair only on the sides of his head. Katherine was looking at him with opened mouth and terror in her eyes. The priest did not say anything out loud, but Sitheia was certain that he was communicating with Katherine who bowed her head with tears in her eyes.

"You should go, Sitheia." Katherine said to Sitheia without raising her head.

Sitheia was about to ask what was going on, but Katherine cut her off.

"Just go, please."

Sitheia was taken aback by Katherine's strange behavior, but then John came from another corridor and joined them so she was ready to leave.

"All right." Sitheia said and went to meet John. "John, what are you doing out here? I thought you were working with the masons?" She said as she walked away from the acolyte.

"We finished." He said looking back toward Katherine. "I assume that you are done as well. Is everything all right?"

"Let's get out of here. I am sick of this place." Sitheia said leading them outside.

They exited the temple as fast as Sitheia was able to

lead them away from that place. Sitheia didn't understand what just happened in there, but she believed that without meaning, she has put Katherine in trouble.

Sitheia was so not in the mood for talking to people or even to be seen by people, so she decided to go around the village. The two of them walked in silence until they neared the woods. From here, they would have to walk around the hill and then they will start to climb toward the tower. At least that was her plan.

If Sitheia was alone, she could have climb the hill from here, but that was a difficult climb accompanied by a lot of bruises and cuts and also Sitheia didn't believe that her clothes can take any more patching up. But, she wasn't in a hurry and she wanted to gather some herbs on the way. She could use the coins. She wanted to buy herself a more sturdy set of clothes before the ones that she was wearing fall off completely.

"You are upset about something." John said.

It was not a question, more like an observation. Was she upset?

"I had a bad dream." Sitheia tried to explain. "I think that it was a nightmare and I have a terrible feeling that I just put Katherine in a lot of troubles."

John picked up a wild chestnut that has fallen under its tree.

"Are we looking for something specific or are we taking

everything that can be used?" He asked.

Sitheia got confused for a second, not sure of what he was talking about. When she looked at the chestnut in his hand she figured that it would be better to get as much as possible if she was to get those new clothes before she lose the ones that she was already wearing.

"Everything. Take as much as possible. If we fill the bags with too much cheap stuff and we find something more expensive, we can always unload some of the cheaper stuff."

John agreed and started scanning the land with his eyes.

"What was the dream about?" He asked while they were working.

Sitheia looked at him wondering if she should say anything to him or not, but she knew that she could trust him not to tell anyone. And since she still hasn't uncovered the meaning of the dream, she figured 'what's the harm'.

"It was dark and it was raining..." She started describing the dream.

John listened carefully while she spoke without interrupting her at all. Sitheia was amazed at how vividly she remembered the dream and the feelings she had while she was having it. As she went into every detail of the dream, she relieved through the entire experience. She was lonely again like when she was talking about being all alone on the rainy night. Sitheia was happy again when she saw the two monsters and worried when they attacked each other. She felt the snow blanketing the meadow at the base of the tower and was horrified when the monsters turned on her. When she finished talking she was almost as sweaty as when she woke up during the night. Thank the Goddess. She was still energized by the ritual of purification.

When she finished describing her dream, she looked at John expecting some kind of comment or question, but he said nothing. He just continued to gather herbs.

"Well? Don't you have anything to say?" Sitheia asked getting annoyed by his silence.

John looked at her at first a little surprised by her outburst. Then he continued to scan the land and spoke at the same time.

"Have you considered that it might be just a dream?" John asked.

"What?" Sitheia was confused.

"I mean… Tonight is your birthday when you officially become an adult. Your family, the rest of Sacred Pools, even the Lords of Perdival, everyone is going to have so much expectations from you. You will have to start providing for yourself and help others as well. That must be very stressful. Don't you think?"

"I didn't, until now." Sitheia said with panic building up in her voice. Suddenly, the realization of what this birthday will mean for her future life become a lot more real than it was until then.

"Maybe you did subconsciously, but you didn't notice because you are always so busy."

"You think so?" Sitheia looked at John who was picking little blue flowers and putting them in his gathering bag. Sitheia always took what John said a little more seriously than if it was coming from anyone else. After all he was hers and he had his best interests at heart.

"Why else would you be dreaming something like that, unless it was your subconsciousness trying to tell you something?" When he said it like that, the whole dream got a totally different perspective, but some things didn't add up and she said that.

"But, some things don't add up. In real life I have never seen a wolf-man or a vampire. They don't live in these areas. All I have heard about either of them is what Mrs. Agnes would tell me whenever she is trying to convince me to wear one of her charms for protection against them. So, there is no reason why I would be dreaming about them, right?"

"Perhaps the wolf-man is not a wolf-man and the vampire is not a vampire." John said.

"Now you've lost me completely." Sitheia raised her hands in frustration.

"Well, you said that you liked the vampire and the

wolf-man. That is not a normal reaction to monsters. Usually people are scared of them, because they are monsters and they prey on humans." John started, but Sitheia interrupted him.

"Yea, but in the second part of the dream, they turned on me."

"Exactly, that can mean that you've been thinking of something that you like, but it's not very good or healthy for you."

"Like what?" Sitheia tried to think of what is that thing that she likes, but is not good for her.

"Like obligations coming from your family and from the community. You love them, your family. But, the expectations that they have for you may not be what you want and that may be draining your health. Things like that can be stressful."

Sitheia considered what John said. She knew why his thoughts have gone to things like family and community, considering that his all life he has been struggling with both. But, being close to the problem didn't necessarily mean that he was wrong.

Starting from tomorrow, both her family and the Cat community will start having expectations from Sitheia. But, the way their community functioned was that as long as she was bringing value to them, they had no say in any of her choices.

They may try to pressure her to go in one direction or another, but ultimately it was her choice. That is, unless she is picked to go to the castle. If that happens, then all bets are off and nothing would be certain after that. But, even if that happens, at least her life will become a lot more interesting. Though, she didn't like the possibility of leaving her family, John and of course her tower.

"How did you feel when you woke up?" John's question pulled her away from her thoughts. She had to think for a second to remember it clearly, but she did.

"I felt like there was something very wrong and somehow it might have been my fault." Sitheia said with a strained voice.

"Your fault? How?" John asked.

"I have no idea. I'm just concerned that it may be like the dreams that my grandma used to have." Sitheia said. Voicing her fear out loud somehow made her feel colder.

Not knowing how to help her, John considered what she said and shrugged.

"You are right. The whole dream doesn't make sense." He said while checking how full his gathering bag is. "Also the meadow at that crumbled old tower. Why would you be dreaming about that? You are not going there any more, right?"

John looked at Sitheia expecting a confirmation which he didn't get. Sitheia pretended to be busy stuffing her bag with all sort of herbs both useful and useless, just so she would have more time to think about the answer. Even better, if she doesn't answer for a while, maybe John will forget that he asked the question in the first place. At least, that is what she was hoping for.

The visits to the tower, Sitheia kept for herself. While John was able to understand more than anyone else about the things that made her so different than any other Cat, he still wasn't happy about her obsession with the Door. He told her that, years ago. He feared that the Door was holding some kind of curse and Sitheia's disregard for the dangers of that place will make her an easy prey to it.

"You are not going there any more, aren't you?" He repeated the question with the beginnings of panic dripping in his voice.

"I… mmm…" Sitheia tried to answer but she didn't want to disappoint him.

"No! Sitty! You know how dangerous that place is." John was scared out of his mind. "Why would you risk going there?"

"Listen, John." Sitheia started to defend her views. "It's OK. The things that you have heard are just stories. They are not true. I go there because it's the most beautiful and most peaceful place in the world. And I need it."

"You need it? That sounds like you are addicted to it. Sitty, that place is evil. I can feel it and I fear that it has a hold over you. What if something happens to you, Sitty? I don't know that I will be able to handle that. I think I'll go insane. Without you, I am nothing. Without you, I am just an empty husk." John said with tears running down his cheeks.

Sitheia couldn't believe that this huge man-mountain made out of muscles was crying. But, he was crying because he was concerned about her safety. She came to him and gave him a hug. He took comfort in the hug, but he was still crying.

"Please, don't cry, John. You know that I care about you. I would never leave you. And it's not true that you are nothing. You are strong and you are smart. You are smarter than me." She stepped away from the hug smiling and pointed to his gathering bag. "Your bag is already full, while mine is not even half way."

John wiped at the tears with his sleeve. He avoided looking at her eyes, but he wasn't feeling any better.

"That place is cursed. I am scared of it."

"That is not true. I've been going there my entire life and nothing bad ever happened to me. In fact, I haven't felt that good anywhere else. Whenever I would feel lonely or sad or frustrated, the Door has always been there to support me. And those tales that people are spreading about the tower, you should know better than to trust the superstitious nonsense that people are saying."

That stopped him for a moment. He truly did know better than to trust the superstations that people were making up. For his entire life, people have been calling him the Last Child, blaming him for not being able to have children for that seven year period. All his life he has been shunned and he has been paying for something that he had no way of influencing or changing. People didn't care that it wasn't his fault for being born, they just needed someone to blame. He swallowed hard before saying anything else.

"I know better. I don't trust a word that anyone else says other than you." John said every word heavy as a boulder. "It's that whenever I have come close to the tower I feel strange. Out of nowhere a sudden wave of dread comes over me. That is a warning. There is something very wrong with that place."

"What do you mean you feel dread?"

"I don't know. Maybe only I feel that way. But, I care about you. For everything that you have done for me and for what you mean to me, I would give my life for you." Every word he said sounded honest to Sitheia. She had no doubt about it. "But, I don't know how to protect you from curses and things that I can't see and are making me scared."

"John, I don't know why you feel like that around the tower, but I assure you I am perfectly safe in there. When I am sitting next to the Door, I feel like I am where I belong. It's hard to describe it, but I feel connection to that place."

She said, and put a finger to his mouth to put an end to the conversation. "Now, let us do what we are here to do before it gets dark. I want to pick some of those white expensive flowers and then we can go back to the village."

Half of the day has already past and the sun has already started to go down when they spotted the flowers that Sitheia was looking for.

"I don't like it here." John said.

True, Sitheia had an ulterior motive for wanting to find these special little flowers. She didn't really have to look for them, because she already knew where these rear flowers grow. Right in front of them was a little green meadow and those tiny little flowers grew next to the giant blocks of stone that have fallen off from the ancient tower that overlooked Sacred Pools like a torch. Sitheia loved this place. Nowhere else she has felt more at home than here.

She turned to look at John. But, his face was pale like a chalk.

"Are you doing all right, John? You don't look so good."

He opened his mouth to answer and closed it down afterward. He looked strange. He did that several times with no words coming from him. He just stared at the tower moving his mouth like a fish out of the water.

"Hey, John!" She yelled at him. He looked at her and blood started to return to his face.

"It's happening, Sitty." He whispered. "I can feel it,

like if I get any closer I'll die."

Sitheia couldn't believe what she was hearing. It didn't make any sense and John was not someone who would be spinning tales. She returned back to him stepping in front of his eyes.

"Look at me!" She said when John tried to return his eyes back to the tower. "It's OK. If you can't come in here, then don't."

She pushed him back a little and watched as color returned to his face. He looked to her like he was waking up from an unpleasant dream.

"When I stood there I felt so scared. I couldn't look away and it felt like death. I felt like I was about to fall in an endless darkness." John said holding his head with both hands. That last part felt familiar to Sitheia, but she couldn't remember from where. "Please, don't make me come any closer. Please, don't make me."

Sitheia was confused by his behavior. She looked over her shoulder toward her beloved tower. With every fiber of her being she loved that place.

'Maybe, you don't want him here? You don't trust him?' She thought not expecting an answer.

She had the habit of talking to the Door whenever she needed to think about something. When she was at the tower she spoke to it directly, at other times she spoke to it in her mind.

"It's all right, John. It's all right. You don't have to go any closer to the tower." She said with a gentle smile on her face. "Why don't you go back to Sacred Pools and sell the herbs to Mrs. Agnes. I'll stay here for a while to gather some of these special herbs and then I'll go back as well."

"You'll stay?" John said sounding scared.

"Yes, I'll stay. I'll be fine. It's just that the tower doesn't trust you, yet."

"Are you sure?"

"I am. Now go."

"OK. I'll see you later."

"It will be late. I'll see you tomorrow." Sitheia said sending him away.

Sitheia just remembered something important.

"Hey, John!" She called after the big man, who turned still looking a little shaken. "You can't tell anyone about this place, neither about the tower nor about me being here. Understand?"

"I won't tell anyone. I swear."

She smiled at him reassuringly one more time and watched him disappear behind a tree. Sitheia turned toward the meadow and took a deep breath. This place, this place was the most beautiful thing that Sitheia has ever dreamed of.

Most girls in the village or better to say almost everyone in her village dream of living in Castle Perdival. She has heard countless stories about lavish dresses and extravagant balls, whatever the word extravagant means. Stories about Lords who duel each other gallantly over the honor of some fair maiden.

Of course, none from Sacred Pools has actually set a foot in the castle and seen any of the things that they were talking about, but they still choose to dream about them. The Cat that went to live there never came back, so they couldn't share stories about the magnificence of living in the castle.

Sitheia was different. When she would daydream, she fantasized about being here, on this meadow. She imagined herself sunbathing in the summer on top of one of those large blocks of stone that are covered with light green moss. Lying on a bed made of soft grass with flowers as her scented pillow, it was just magical. She would fantasize that she is seating next to her friend at the end of the spiral stairs even on a cold snowy day. Here she knew that she is safe. This is where she is always welcome. This little corner of the world belonged to her.

Sitheia smiled feeling good and went up to greet her friend.

CHAPTER 6

Sitheia sat next to the giant door that was the entrance to the ancient ruins that hunted her curiosity since she was able to walk. Among her first memories from the world outside her parents' home was walking unsteadily over the threshold and looking up over the roof of their neighbor's house. It was the first time she saw the shape of the tower in the distance. A giant tower on top of the hill that seemed like someone was holding a torch over the valley. To Sitheia it was like a hand waving at her calling her to come and play.

Sitheia looked at her silent friend. The Door looked the same as always, never moving, never changing. The Door was the only visible entrance to the ancient half ruined tower. Once, long time ago there may have been other entrances into the tower, now there are only broken old blocks of stone that blocked everything else.

The only thing on this tower that wasn't ruined was the spiral staircase that went all around the tower up to the place where Sitheia was sitting right now. It was a pretty door with all sorts of carvings on it.

She could clearly remember the first time she met her friend. Her father, George Cat was a hunter and his father was a hunter before him and his father before him and so on for generations. Her father knew the woods by heart and felt that it was his duty to introduce the beauty of the forest to his daughter.

Which is why, one morning when she was six years old, they both got dressed and ready for her first venture into the forest. Her mother, Mary Cat has made her a little gathering bag that she can wear over her shoulder. It was a miniature version of the one that Sitheia used now. But, then at the age of six, it made her feel like a real hunter.

Her father had it all planned out. They walked along the river for a while and he was teaching her the entire time about what hunters are doing and why. Even now Sitheia remembered his lessons as if she could hear her father speaking right in front of her.

The most important rule was: We hunt so we can eat, we don't kill what we don't have to. Respect the land

and she will provide you with everything that you need to survive. He showed her where to look for animals, how to track them and how to catch them. He showed her how to stay hidden and move like a cat which was funny to Sitheia because their people were also called the Cat.

Later when it was almost noon, her father had caught a pheasant and they were ready to go home. A strong wind started blowing from the hill overlooking the village. It was at that moment that Sitheia heard it, the call.

"Sitheia."

"Sitheia."

It was like a whisper that traveled with the wind. Her father didn't hear anything, but she did. Without him noticing, Sitheia walked into the forest away from the river. She had no idea where she was going. She just followed the guidance of the wind. And then she stumbled upon the most beautiful green meadow filled with tiny little white flowers that smelled amazing. At the other side of the meadow she saw the big stone blocks with tops covered in green moss that she loved to hug even today. Slightly to the side she noticed the stairs that went up into a spiral around the tower.

There were no railings for her hands and the wind was strong, but she was not afraid. Even when she looked over the edge and saw that it was the highest that she has ever been, even then she was not afraid of falling. On top of the stairs there was a small landing platform and there it was, the Door.

She has stared at the Door for so long that she knew every inch of it by heart. Sitheia could trace the carvings on the giant door in her mind without looking.

"Hello. I am Sitheia, but everyone calls me Sitty." Those were the first of many words that her six years old version has spoken to the Door.

Like every other time after that encounter, the conversations were one-sided. But, if you ask Sitheia, she would say that they were having amazing conversations. Sitheia thought that the Door spoke through the wind, because obviously she didn't have a mouth. Whether that was true or not, it didn't matter to George when he came to the tower calling for her breathless and pale.

"Sitty! Sitty! Where are you?!"

Sitheia was so drawn to the Door that she didn't hear her father calling until he was at the foot of the stairs. When she heard him calling, she called back.

"Daddy! Daddy! Look what I found!"

The scared father almost run up the stairs and nearly fell of the edge until he laid his eyes on the girl. The moment he saw her, he grabbed her immediately and hugged her so tight.

"Don't ever do that again. I thought that you were lost. When we go into the woods, we stay together." George said looking around at the place where he has found her. "And we never come here. It takes just a small slip of the foot and you can fall of the edge."

"But, dad. Look what I found. She is so beautiful." Sitheia said still in her father's hug.

He pulled back from the hug so he can see what she was showing to him. As a hunter, he knew the stories about this place and none of them were good. Not wanting to scare the girl when they were still at such a dangerous place, he took her by her hand saying.

"Come Sitty, it's getting cold and your mother will be worried. We should be getting back."

"What's inside, dad?" Sitheia asked starting to walk reluctantly.

"I don't know. No one does. It has been sealed for hundreds of years at least. It can't be opened."

Sitheia turned to look at the Door for the last time before her father pulled her down the stairs.

"That's all right." Little Sitheia said. "She doesn't have to open. I can tell. We are going to be friends."

Her father just shook his head and started to lead her down the stairs. Sitheia didn't protest getting off the tower. After all she found what she was looking for, a friend.

"I'll see you later." She whispered at the Door.

After that first visit of the tower, Sitheia had trouble getting anywhere near it for a while. When she was out with her father, he always paid close attention to her whereabouts and he would never let her wonder off on her own like that again. It made her sad that she can't see the Door again. She asked questions about it constantly and some people from the village who liked to tell stories had some of the answers.

Mr. Olaf, the innkeeper told her that the Door was magically sealed hundreds of years ago and that it would not budge even if you try to break it down with hammers and axes. People used to come from all over the country trying to get inside hoping to find treasures and riches. Unsuccessfully, of course. There were many who have tried to hack the Door to pieces who ended up with broken axes.

Others tried to burn it down. The story says that no flame ever touched the Door and the people who have tried to set it on fire were blown away by the wind. They have fallen some sixty feet onto the rocks under the tower breaking every bone in their bodies.

The one that Sitheia liked the most was the story about the Lord who came from Starcross City with a battering ram trying to break it down. In the end the battering ram couldn't take the battering and fell apart, while the Door remained untouched. Sitheia couldn't stop laughing whenever she would hear this one.

The attempts to open the Door ended when several hundreds of years ago the Lord of Perdival from that age hired a wizard to come and inspect the Door. The wizard has returned down the stairs running with face pale from fear. He told everyone to stay away from that door. He told them that it has been magically sealed and with a good reason. Behind the Door, there was a terrible curse.

Sitheia personally didn't take this last story about the Door too seriously unlike everyone else. She has spent half of her life near the Door and she has never seen anything strange that might make her belief that the place was cursed. For Sitheia, the place was just magical.

She was almost ten when she sneaked through the wheat fields and got at the bottom of the rocky hill underneath the tower. She could no longer wait for her hunts with her father hoping that she will be able to sneak to the meadow. Looking up, she had no doubt that it was a difficult climb, especially for a ten year old child that has never climbed anything taller than a tree. Sitheia could remember the wind blowing the entire time while she was climbing the rocks and she wasn't scared that the wind will blow her off the hill. No. On the contrary, she felt like she was much lighter and she climbed a lot easier.

When she finally pulled herself on the meadow at the base of the tower and she climbed up the spiral stairs to the landing platform on top, she was all scratched and her clothes were torn in so many places that she worried that her parents might be mad at her. But, looking in front of her, she saw the Door standing grand and amazing like one of those murals inside the temple of the Goddess. Sitheia immediately felt a connection with the place.

As Sitheia was growing she came often to visit her friend. She would sit at the edge of the stairs and would talk to the Door for hours. Her silent friend never answered, but at least there was someone who listened to her. John loved to listen to her talking and could just stand there and listen to her all day, but it was not the same. Her connection to the Door was different, stronger.

For all the years that Sitheia have spent sitting by the Door and talking to her, not once she tried to open the locked door that was keeping her company so often while she was growing into a young woman. She didn't care whether the Door would open or not, she was happy that it was there and that she could talk to it for hours never to be judged for being different than the rest.

Sitheia loved to sit on the edge of the spiral stairs looking down at the stones at the bottom of the cliff. She loved the view from this high and she never got dizzy. From here, Sitheia could see so much more of the world then she ever could from her home. From here, the entire valley was opened to her eyes.

From up here, Sitheia could see the roof of her home. Even at this distance she could see the fires of the blacksmith's forge right behind her family house. The roaring fires of the blacksmith's forge were often all that she could see in the evenings when she would forget herself and return home late. There, right next to her home was the house where John lived with his parents.

The river that passed through the village and the mill working on logs were always making a lot of noise. Further away toward the center of the village was the large home of the Village Elder where he and his most trusted advisors lived with their families. At the center of the village was the Inn. By the purple smoke coming out of the chimney, Sitheia recognized the Alchemist's Hut where Mrs. Agnes lived.

Outside the village to the right, Sitheia could see the rocky slopes of the White Mountain that were always covered in snow. Sitheia tried to imagine what the view would look like from there. She thought about it for a while before she answered herself. She probably wouldn't be able to see anything. There was a reason why the mountain was called the White Mountain. It was always snowing up there, as it was another world completely separated from theirs and they were only looking at it through a window. Even in the middle of summer when in Sacred Pools was hot enough for people to wish that they were fish because they would always live in water. Even then, on the mountain snowed as the inside of a snow globe.

Far behind the White Mountain was the capital, the

great Starcross City. Sitheia have heard tales about heroes who lived there and the magnificence of the buildings where the streets were made of smooth stone blocks instead of dirt. She wanted to see it one day. At least she used to until today's lesson.

Sitheia wanted to see any place other than Sacred Pools. She believed that her home and her village were rich and beautiful and she truly believed that their lives were blessed, but she couldn't help herself. Sitheia was curious by nature and she wanted to see new things and new places.

One of the many alluring things about this tower was that from up here she could see so much further than the village that was her entire world. That made her believe that there are so many opportunities out there and she wasn't bound to Sacred Pools forever.

When Sitheia spent time on the tower's staircase looking at the only world that she knew, her favorite place to rest her eyes was on the left side. Far down the river, after a small forest there was a gorgeous looking beach. Sitheia couldn't see it from here, but she has heard stories that the beach was covered with grains of sand that were as small and tiny as flour. She has never been there and she has never seen the sea from up close, but she could hear the waves and the wind would occasionally bring the smell of salt.

It was a bit of a distance, but she could see the small

island in the sea along with the castle, the tall walls and towers just like in the bedtime stories her mother told her when she was a little girl. Sitheia imagined the elegantly dressed people dancing in beautiful gowns at one of their fancy balls. That castle was Castle Perdival where the lords who owned the village and the surrounding area lived. Her village along with a neighboring village was a fief to the Lord of Perdival. She has never seen him, none in her village have. But, occasionally they would see emissaries from the castle visiting the village or one of their trading carts would pass through the village filled to the brim with marvelous goods.

Sitheia was always impressed with how the Lords of Perdival were dressed. Clean and smooth in nice colors and no holes in their clothes or boots. She often wondered how come they were not feeling cold when all of their fancy clothes looked to be quite thin, but her father has told her their secret.

"Look closer." He whispered once when the emissaries were in the village. "Do you see the glow that is coming from their outfit?"

Little Sitheia looked intently trying not to blink and she saw that the dark red vest really did have a faint glow.

"What is it?" She asked her father.

"It's enchanted, child." He told her with a knowing smile.

As much as she was impressed by the pretty clothes, the stern expressions on the beautiful faces and the elegant weaponry, always made her feel intimidated by the Lords of Perdival. That is why she kept her distance whenever they would be visiting Sacred Pools.

Sitheia was disappointed that the sun was starting to go down. But, she knew what day was today. It was the first day of spring, it was her birthday. Tonight she was coming of age. It was a big day, bigger than any of her previous birthdays. In the eyes of the world, her village and her family she was no longer a child. Her mother would be baking a pie. Sitheia has seen her mother and her sister preparing the apples before she left the house that morning. She smiled, apple pie was her favorite.

Sitheia looked toward the Door that stood the same, magically beautiful just like the first time she saw it. There were not a lot of people in Sacred Pools that were close to her age. So, this door had a greater role in her life growing up, it was more like a silent friend than a place to escape to. She got up, dusted her clothes, said "see you tomorrow" to her friend and started climbing off the tower.

CHAPTER 7

As Sitheia walked over the bridge she was yet again amazed by how the sun seemed to always be finding a way to avoid their village. She knew that it was early for the sun to go down, but it was cloudy enough that the villagers had to ignite the lanterns on their porches.

Sitheia never enjoyed walking over the large dirt street. She always felt kind of exposed, like everyone was watching her and measuring her worth. She didn't like being measured. Several houses ahead, right in front of the elder's house there were four horses and one elegantly dressed person. "One of the Lords" she thought.

She had no reason to be avoiding them. It was more of a reflex. Sitheia made a quick turn to the right and she was circling behind the house of the baker. Everyone were intimidated by their masters, the Lords of Perdival, so Sitheia thought that sneaking away from them wasn't particularly cowardly from her. Just around two more backyards and she would be home and she will be celebrating.

"Rarrrrr! I'm gonna eat you! Rarrr!" Sitheia heard interesting sounds right ahead.

She saw children playing on the street close to her house. Some of the children had put on sheepskins since they didn't have wolf skins over their heads and were pretending to be werewolves. While other children have made small masks out of chicken bones that looked like large fangs and they were pretending to be vampires. Sitheia's younger sister and two other kids were in a third group playing to be scared humans.

Sitheia recognized the game that they were playing. It was the story about the battle between vampires and werewolves with the humans caught in the middle. The innkeeper Mr. Olaf has been telling that story since she could remember. Sitheia was never able to play the game. When she was little, the older kids didn't want to play with her because they were much older. In turn when she got older herself, she didn't want to play with kids so much younger than she was.

She sort of adopted John much later when she was no longer interested in playing games. She tried several times in her head to imagine how it would look like if she was playing the game. It never worked. She could never decide on which side to play, they all seemed interesting to be like, but also they all seemed somehow wrong.

There was a cry and all the kids suddenly got very quiet pulling Sitheia out of her thoughts. She got startled. She saw a tall, beautiful and dangerous looking woman dressed in fine clothes with armor and weapon that looked to be made more for fashion than for warfare. She was one of the Lords of Perdival.

It seemed that one of the boys pretending to be a vampire wasn't looking where he was running and he bumped into her. The reaction of the Lady of Perdival was slapping the boy out of her way. Sitheia has seen her before, she didn't know her name, but she was as ruthless as she was stunningly beautiful. The woman looked down at the child that was clutching its cheek, with the chicken bone mask still on its face. Sitheia could swear that she saw a twitch in the woman's lips.

"Now, what are you supposed to be?" She asked the boy, which was too afraid to look anywhere else but at her feet.

"A vampire, my lord…mmm… my lady." The child mumbled.

"Are you now?" She smirked. "You should be more careful of where you are going, child. Others might not be as forgiving as I am."

"I am sorry, my lady. Thank you, my lady." The child tried to hide his tears.

The child was obviously no longer on the woman's mind because she was already on her way. Sitheia was hidden behind a tree for the entire event making sure that she wasn't seen by anyone.

As the Lady disappeared from her line of sight, Sitheia let go of her breath that she didn't even realized that she was holding. All the emissaries, both the men and the women had some amazing ability to make her feel like she was in love and like she was scared for her life at the same time. Even though in her entire life, not one of them has ever acknowledged her existence. But this Lady was exceptional and Sitheia didn't want to find herself face to face with her. She gave her the creeps.

With the Lady gone, the children scurried away to their homes and Sitheia was ready to come out from behind the tree and head home when she remembered that Mrs. Agnes, the herbalist was expecting her.

CHAPTER 8

The Alchemist's Hut was a very tiny shack with misty windows. From outside it was impossible to imagine how anything can fit into that tiny place.

People walking by would often start coughing. Mostly that was because of all the puffs of smoke in various colors that came out of every crack that could be found. Smoke in green, violet, orange and every other color that exists except for grey was coming out of the chimney that was a little crooked, from an open window or from a loose floorboard. Sitheia used to joke that the house was smoking tobacco and that was the reason for all the smoke.

Mrs. Agnes lived and worked in her shop like most of the people in the village. She was a woman of many talents.

People called her an alchemist, even though she preferred to be called herbalist. She gathered herbs and brew potions for all sorts of ailments and afflictions. Some potions were more effective than others.

Her potions could heal things like common cold, a cough, and a snotty nose. She prepared poultices for bruises and cuts, and creams and lotions for sore joints and pulled muscles. But, she was also very good at making rat poisons or scents for the lures that the hunters and the fishermen were using. Most people for healing preferred to use her medicines rather than going through the dangerous ritual at the temple.

After the previous midwife was taken to work at the castle, Mrs. Agnes took over the role of a midwife as well.

Sitheia joked that all she needed to be a proper witch was an owl and a pointy hat. Mrs. Agnes thought that Sitheia was funny and she never took offense.

For the people of Sacred Pools, Agnes was a very important person. They appreciated her work and valued her presence in the village and that was not a small feat for someone who was not a Cat. During the past several hundred years, Agnes was the only person who lived in the village who was not born in Sacred Pools.

Even after years of living in the village among the Cat people, the people of Sacred Pools still treated Agnes as a valued guest and would often bring her a basket of fruits, freshly baked bread, a pie or even a freshly caught fish or a small animal.

Sitheia liked Agnes. The herbalist had an aura about her of intelligence and mystery that the impressionable girl admired. Agnes was also very witty and it was easy for her to make Sitheia burst into laughter.

Once the herbalist learned that the girl has a habit of taking strolls through the woods, she made sure that Sitheia is not coming back empty handed. It wasn't long before Agnes suggested that while Sitheia was in the forest, she can look for various herbs and flowers that she needed for her potions.

Agnes wasn't young and she didn't know the land as well as Sitheia did, so she didn't know where to find all the herbs that she needed. The herbalist was also more than happy to pay Sitheia for every herb that she would bring to her which was the only motivation that the ambitious Sitheia needed.

At first Sitheia didn't know anything about herbs and couldn't make the difference between a mint leaf and walnut. All she knew was where certain colors grew. But, after several times she brought to Agnes a bunch of useless weeds, roots and all, the herbalist figured that it would be better for her if she teaches the girl few things about the various herbs and their properties.

Sitheia learned that from some plants she only needed

to pick the leaves, from others the flower, while from third she needed the root. There were also some special herbs where the whole plant was useful only for very different purposes. One part of the plant could kill you while another part of the same plant could save your life.

After Sitheia got blisters on her fingers from touching the leaves of a nettle, she started to wear leather gloves that her mother has made for her. It wasn't long that Sitheia figured out that not all herbs have the same value. Some were more common and could easily be found in larger quantities, these plants were cheap and Sitheia wasn't very fond of them.

Her favorites were the ones that were very rear and could only be found in some places that were not very accessible or were too dangerous for anyone without the required skillset. These herbs brought her a lot of coins and also finding them was always a lot of fun because they grew in the most interesting places. The flower that she picked at the tower earlier today was one of those rear herbs.

When Sitheia pushed the door open and stepped into the shop she hit her head on a wreath made of garlic. A bell above the door rang.

"Ouch!" She ducked doing her best not to catch her hair on one of the many circular platters that hung on chains from the beams on the ceiling. The platters were all covered with neatly laid herbs left to dry.

Sitheia looked around the shop looking for the herbalist but she could hardly see anything from all the stuff that was everywhere. She stared at the room for a moment and then stepped out of the shop again. She looked at the building measuring it with her eyes before she reentered the shop.

'Wow. This shop is a test for sanity.' She thought. She had no idea how it was possible for all the things that were inside to be stuffed in a place that at least from outside wasn't that big.

Sitheia also could never understand how can there be so many things stuffed in such a small place. There were cabinets on top of cabinets filled with vials in various colors. There were pots everywhere and Sitheia was sure that somewhere there was a fireplace but she could never see it. She assumed that the fireplace must be in the backroom since the place was always warm and there was smoke coming out of the chimney, so there must be one, even though she has never seen it.

"Sitty? Is that you girl?" A female voice came from behind a curtain that leads to the backroom. The curtain looked so stained that you could say that it was artfully painted.

"It's me, Mrs. Agnes," called Sitheia.

A woman in her late forties entered the shop from behind the counter wiping her hands on a piece of cloth towel. The woman, Agnes, looked like everyone's favorite aunt. She always had a smile and a pleasant word for everyone making the person that she was talking to feel like the most important person in the world.

"Why do you keep that thing over the front door? I am hitting my head every time I come in." Sitheia complained while carefully she was making progress toward the counter.

"Sitty, I've kept a wreath made of garlic over there for almost fifteen years. By now, you should have gotten used to it and learned how to avoid it as a reflex. Beside it is foolish not to have one over your front door. It protects against vampires."

"With that much garlic it protects against people too," Sitheia rolled her eyes and closed her nose with two fingers to make a point.

"Very clever. You shouldn't roll your eyes, Sitty or they will get stuck like that." Agnes smiled at the girl. "If it was up to me, every home would have one over their front door."

"Mrs. Agnes? But, what if the vampire sneaks through the window?" Sitheia teased brushing a strand of hair from her face.

"Feel free to take a look," Agnes pointed toward the window.

Sitheia carefully approached the window not sure how much garlic she was going to see. But, on the window there wasn't a wreath of garlic. Instead, there was a single garlic clove tied to half an apple and several leaves of laurel. Sitheia couldn't help herself and rolled her eyes again making Agnes laugh and say.

"You should take the creatures of darkness a lot more seriously."

"I do, I swear."

Sitheia wasn't lying. Last night was not the first time she had a dream about vampires and werewolves. Since she was very little she's been having violent nightmares about battles between vampires and werewolves. Her mom said that it was a result of the stories that Mr. Olaf the innkeeper and her grandfather Peter were telling her. Last night's dream really freaked her out, it felt way too real.

"Are you all right, Sitty? You look a little pale." Agnes looked concerned.

"I am fine. I just had a bad dream and it's been bothering me a little." Sitheia at the same time wanted to share her dream, but she doubted that Mrs. Agnes would understand her situation.

"A dream? About what?" The herbalist fixed Sitheia with her look.

Sitheia wanted to tell Agnes everything about the dream, about the Door, but she couldn't. The Door was her special place, her secret and no one could know about their relationship. As for the dream, she doubted that anyone could be of help. Her conversation with John helped a little, but he was always more attuned to her. She didn't want the herbalist to judge her.

"It was about a giant mushroom with bulging eyes." Sitheia remembered the joke that Katherine made. Agnes was bewildered.

"A mushroom with bulging eyes?" Agnes repeated. "How on earth are you managing to invent these things?" The herbalist said while shaking her head.

"I don't know. It's not like I want to dream of crazy stuff like that." Sitheia said defensively. "It was just a silly dream."

"Silly, indeed." Agnes agreed. "But, that doesn't make the creatures of darkness any less real and dangerous."

"I know that they are real and that they are dangerous, but don't they all live far to the southeast part of the continent. We don't have any vampires in these parts. So why worry over something that exists on the other side of the world."

"Oh, sometimes you amaze me at how naive you are." said Agnes. "Your pet, John was here earlier."

Sitheia's face turned as red as a ripe tomato shocked by the sudden change of topic.

"Mrs. Agnes! I can't believe you just said that." She said furiously.

"Oh, what did I said?" Agnes asked pretending not to understand where the problem was.

"John is not my pet. He is…"

"He follows you around. He is doing everything you tell him. You are not feeding him, yet. But, otherwise, I don't see where I've made a mistake. He is almost like Miss. Olivia."

"Who's Miss. Olivia? He is not my pet. He needs me… It's not his fault… for being born. I care about him, because no one else does. And that is a loss for everyone else, because he has so much potential in him." Sitheia spoke confidently and with conviction.

"I am sorry, girl. I did not mean to insult John. I know that he is a good lad." Agnes said kindly. "I was just messing with you. But, I am glad that you are so passionate about protecting what is yours. You are not mad at me, are you?"

"Of course not. I am just tired of everyone underestimating and mistreating John. When I hear someone speaks bad things about him, I just want to punch them all in the face." Sitheia said furiously.

"Oh, I would love to see that." Agnes said laughing.

A noise of some pots falling down and crushing from an unknown location attracted Sitheia's attention.

"What was that?" She asked craning her neck trying to locate the source of the noise.

"Oh, don't worry about that. It's just Miss. Olivia, my cat." Agnes said offhandedly while bending over and looking for something under the counter.

Sitheia has been visiting Agnes for years and she has never seen this cat before or any other cat for that matter.

"She is probably chasing rats." Agnes added.

Sitheia had trouble closing her mouth.

"You have rats?"

"Everyone does. Didn't you know that?"

"No. And since when do you have a cat?"

The domesticated animal that had the same name as her people was not common for Sacred Pools. In fact before this evening Sitheia could swear that there was not a single cat in the entire village.

"Since forever. Come on Sitty, you must have seen Miss. Olivia before." Agnes said from under the counter.

"No, never." Sitheia said trying to remember if she has ever seen this so called Miss. Olivia. "Is this cat real, or did you conjured it with magic?"

"Ha, ha, I'm a witch, very funny." Agnes said sarcastically.

"You know that this may be the first actual cat that has appeared in the village where Cat people live?"

"Oh, I haven't thought much about that." Agnes shrugged.

When the noise finally stopped, out of the backroom came out what was the first cat that Sitheia has ever seen. Miss. Olivia had fur as black as the feathers of a raven and her eyes were glowing red in the shadows as two burning embers. Sitheia wasn't sure if all cats look like Miss. Olivia. Regardless, she felt chills going down her spine.

"What are you looking for down there?" Sitheia asked as she watched the cat disappear behind some boxes on the floor.

"Ah, there it is." Agnes pulled herself up holding a little box in one hand while dusting her clothes with the other. "You didn't think that I will forget did you?"

"What are you talking about?" Sitheia was confused. Agnes looked at her to see if Sitheia was playing smart.

"Have you forgotten what day is today, child? But, wait. You are not a child any longer, are you? Happy birthday, Sitty."

"Oh, thank you." Sitheia said happy to hear the first congratulations for her birthday.

Agnes gave her a hug and she pulled a sweetroll from the box and handed it to her. It was fresh. The doorbell rang.

"Did I hear it right or do my ears deceive me? This young lady becomes of age tonight?" A voice came from the door.

Sitheia and Agnes got startled. They did not notice that the front door of the shop was opened and on its doorstep stood Lord Gavin, one of Perdival's emissaries.

As soon as Sitheia laid her eyes on the Lord, she blushed and she quickly lowered her head to hide her embarrassment. Lord Gavin was probably three or four times her age but she couldn't be around him without blushing. All of Perdival's emissaries had similar effect on her with their perfect pale skin and clean ironed clothes.

The women of Sacred Pools made sure that their clothes were always clean and that they look decent, but ironing clothes was not a common thing. Sitheia has never seen anyone in her village iron their clothes unless it was for a wedding, a funeral or some other equally special event. Even then, it was only a handful of people who did that. There was just no time and no point in doing it.

Sitheia could count on one hand the number of women from Sacred Pools that she has seen to use makeup of any kind. But, every emissary from the castle always had a ton of makeup at all times, with powdered skin that made them look as if they had not a single wrinkle or mark on their skin. The female emissaries had their lips painted with various colors that you can spot from a great distance and their cheeks were covered with so many red, pink or violet dots as if they were blushing at all times. It was like they would burst into flames if they didn't look perfectly beautiful and stunning all the time.

As soon as Agnes and Sitheia noticed the emissary they both made a deep bow.

"Lord Gavin." Agnes acknowledged the emissary. "Welcome to my humble shop, at your service as always."

Lord Gavin stepped into the shop followed by two other emissaries. The Lady that Sitheia saw earlier on the street was on his left side and another Lord who looked to be only slightly older than Sitheia was on his right.

He had a short blond hair and looked very similar to John, only he looked perfect, without any flaws. And where John radiated insecurity and despite his size he always appeared to be very small, this blond emissary was the opposite. He radiated strength and stability as if he was a living moving mountain, but on his face Sitheia could see an expression of an old pain that he has somehow learned to live with it. That pain on his face so much resembled her own John that she wanted to go to him and give him a hug and to tell him that everything was going to be OK. But, he being an emissary meant that she couldn't move, or speak, or even look him in the eyes without her falling apart.

"Lady Erika, Prince Marcus, welcome." Agnes repeated the bow and Sitheia followed.

"Agnes, it is so lovely to see you again." Lord Gavin smiled at the herbalist. The other two did not spoke, they only nodded in acknowledgement.

Sitheia was certain that the face of Mrs. Agnes had the color of ripe tomato. She was pleased that it wasn't just her having problem with being around the Lords.

"But, did I hear it right? Is your birthday tonight? Are

you really coming of age tonight?"

Not one of the many Lords of Perdival that Sitheia has seen during her life has ever acknowledged her existence in any way. In fact not one of them has ever even looked in her direction, even by accident. So much that she feared that she was invisible to their eyes. But now, to be actually addressed by one of them directly, that was shocking and confusing.

Sitheia fearfully looked at the emissaries. Lord Gavin was looking at her with a genuine interest. Lady Erika had her fixed with her narrowed eyes that made her gulp. The last emissary, the Prince, the pain on his face was almost unbearable for Sitheia to look at. It took her a moment to realize that everyone was looking at her expecting an answer.

"Yes... my lord... tonight is my birthday... - Sitheia managed to push the words out of her mouth. She was certain that if her mother saw her mumbling like this to a Lord that she would be mortified."

"Now, isn't that a wondrous moment in a person's life. There are many birthdays in one's life, but none as special as this one. This is the birthday when the child is left behind and an adult person emerges to the benefit of the world."

Sitheia was amazed how did Lord Gavin managed to say so much, but to do it in such an elegant way. His lips barely moved keeping the perfection of his face intact. She was almost dazed by the lack of movement from his lips.

Lord Gavin was obviously feeling merciful because he left the poor girl to herself and addressed the herbalist instead.

"Agnes. You know why I am here."

"Of course, my lord" Agnes wiped her hands again from her towel.

"I assume that you have them ready." Sitheia found it amazing at how every word that Lord Gavin was saying sounded like a statement on the verge of command, even though it should have sounded like a question.

"Of course, my lord. Here they are, just as you asked."

Agnes pulled a heavy basket filled with tiny purple bottles arranged carefully in straw so they wouldn't break.

"I made a batch for at least two months," Agnes was beaming, proud of her work.

Lord Gavin signaled the Prince who took the basket in one hand and inspected the bottles. Sitheia found it impressive that the Prince held the basket with ease with only one hand while Agnes was having trouble with both hands. He must be very strong. She also noticed that while John's hair was mostly a dark shade of blond, more like the color of honey, the Prince's hair was a bright blonde color like the shine of a winter's sun. Sitheia shook her head forcing herself to snap out of the daze.

After the Prince gave a nod, Lord Gavin pulled a small

pouch from his belt and gave it to the herbalist. Sitheia guessed that the pouch was filled with coins. Agnes took the pouch and thanked the Lord repeatedly while bowing several times. She did not open it to look inside. Sitheia guessed that that might have been perceived as an insult by the emissaries.

The emissaries were getting ready to leave the shop and they have just turned toward the exit, when she couldn't take it anymore. The pain on his face, she could almost feel it as her own. Sitheia didn't know what made her do it, but she opened her mouth to speak even though she regretted before the words came out.

"Excuse me, my lord." She said with a nervous voice that had a lot higher tone than her normal voice.

The emissaries turned to look at her and Agnes was also staring at her. It was not a common thing for anyone to address one of the Lords of Perdival unless they were spoken to.

"Forgive me, my lord, my prince for speaking out of turn." Her eyes met with the light blue eyes of the Prince. An expression of confusion and a bit of surprise got mixed in with the pain. "I wondered… I wondered if you needed something for the pain. A potion perhaps?"

The Prince's eyes doubled in size from surprise. The other two emissaries while also surprised, their eyes seemed focused on Sitheia. She felt as if she was being measured.

She should have kept her mouth shut. Talking without thinking was what always got her into trouble. After a very uncomfortable moment, the eyes of Lord Gavin and Lady Erika turned toward their third companion.

"My prince, this girl asked if you needed a potion for your pain." Lord Gavin addressed the Prince. It sounded polite, but to Sitheia it felt a little too sharp to be polite.

As the Prince was looking at Sitheia, his eyes narrowed for a moment and she got scared that he might be angry with her for overstepping her place, but then his face relaxed. All the pain that she has seen earlier dissipated from it. Even a small smile appeared on his generally serious features.

"Thank you, my lady for your concern. But, it is not necessary. I am feeling well." He said to her and she couldn't help but smile.

With that interruption being settled, the emissaries were ready to exit the shop. Before exiting into the night, Lord Gavin turned one more time toward Sitheia.

"What is your name, girl?"

The question caught Sitheia off guard, so she stuttered.

"Sitty, my lord. I mean Sitheia, but people call me Sitty, my lord."

Lord Gavin smiled sympathetically at her confusion.

"Sitheia." He decided to accept her full name rather than the diminutive version of it. "Happy birthday Sitheia. Do your best to learn as much as you can and one day you may be of use to the castle. The future may have interesting plans for you."

He smiled at her and gave signal to his companions to exit the shop. Just before he was about to duck so he won't hit his head on the garlic wreath, he turned toward Agnes.

"For vampires?" He inquired.

"Of course, my lord. You can never be too careful."

"Of course, garlic. Good thinking." He said, ducked under the wreath and disappeared into the night.

For several minutes the two of them were quiet still stunned by the presence of the Lords. Agnes recovered first.

"Easy, Sitty. Breathe, breathe." The herbalist teased Sitheia once she was sure that there was no one to overhear them.

Sitheia found a three legged stool and sat down doing her best to calm her breathing.

"You do know that if they find something of value for you to do, they may pick you to go and live in the castle. If that happens, you will be seeing them every day. You can't faint every time one of them passes nearby or talks to you."

"I didn't faint." Sitheia protested.

"Almost." Agnes pushed the sweetroll toward her. "Eat it, the sugar will give you energy and will calm you down."

Sitheia ate her sweetroll silently while she saw the encounter with the Lords of Perdival again in her mind.

"Wait, didn't you call that blond Lord a Prince?"

"Yes. That was Prince Marcus. He is the youngest son of Lord Perdival."

"But, if he was a Prince… Why did he…?" Sitheia was trying to focus her thoughts.

"What about him?" Agnes prompted.

"Well, it seemed like Lord Gavin was in charge. If he was a Prince, wouldn't that means that he would outrank Lord Gavin?"

Agnes smiled at the way Sitheia's thoughts were moving.

"It's not that simple. As I said, he is the youngest son. He has eleven older brothers and seven older sisters. Being a Prince for him means that he is nineteenth in line to inherit the throne of Perdival. Lord Gavin is one of the high ranking officers of Lord Perdival. He has been by his side for a very long time and he would certainly outrank most of the Princes and Princesses."

The herbalist pulled another stool and sat close to Sitheia.

"Tell me, what possessed you to say that to the Prince? And how did you even know that he was in pain?" Agnes asked looking inquisitively at the girl who still seemed to be a little distracted.

"Didn't you?" Sitheia asked a little confused, but Agnes just shook her head in response. "It seemed obvious to me. He wasn't hurt physically or anything like that. He reminded me so much of John. I felt that I have to offer him some help. You understand that, right?" Sitheia looked at Agnes hoping for an approval or at least understanding, but she didn't get any of that from the herbalist.

"No Sitty, I don't understand. Every person that is born in that castle is trained about how to hide everything real that is going on inside under that mask made of makeup. And you are telling me that you managed to see past that mask of theirs and you saw a broken spirit like the one in John? That is hard to believe."

Sitheia took several deep breaths, trying to focus her thoughts.

"I didn't say that. I saw that he was feeling pain, very strong pain, a pain that he had for a very long time. But, I didn't say that he was broken."

"And don't. The Lords of Perdival are not to be messed with."

"And what you said about John." Sitheia continued.

"What about him?"

"He is not broken, not any more. Maybe he never was broken, he was just a little lost." Sitheia explained it. She didn't like when anyone was saying bad things about her John. "Then he found me and now he is whole again." She ended with a smile.

"He is lucky to have found you." Agnes pointed.

"We both are lucky to have found each other."

"That is true. Most people don't understand that, but the relationship between a master and a subject goes in both directions." said Agnes.

Sitheia had no comment for that, so she changed the subject.

"Wait. You said something earlier that I wanted to ask you about. What do you mean by that "the Throne of Perdival"? I thought that Lord Perdival was Lord of Castle Perdival, our village. I think that one more village also belonged to him and the surrounding land. But, what I thought was that this entire land was part of the territory of the King of Starcross City."

"Good. Someone paid attention to her history lessons. What you just said is all true on a map. But in real life things are not that simple. The Lord Perdival regularly sends emissaries to every part of the kingdom and they trade with every city of the kingdom. But, have you ever seen an outsider come in these parts, apart from myself? These lands are hidden so well that they are very difficult to find. I suspect that the King of Starcross City is not aware that he has lands and subjects in this part of the world. I may go as far as to suggest that he doesn't even know that these lands even exist."

"So, how did it happen that you came to Sacred Pools?" Sitheia asked.

"I was invited, of course. That is the only way for

someone who has never been here to find this place." Agnes answered like it was obvious.

As a child Sitheia has heard the story of how the Cat people have asked Lord Perdival for protection in exchange for their servitude. Despite her lessons, she never really understood how deep that protection went. Have the Lords of Perdival been really hiding the existence of the Cat people for all these years.

Why would someone hate her people so much that would make the Cat people rather live in servitude than to face their wrath? If long time ago before the Cat name was even used, some ancestors of her people have caused a grievance to someone, not even the ashes from their bones remains now. Who and why would someone be holding a grudge for so long? And that thing that acolyte Nigel said about demons…

"You do know that your face gets all wrinkled when you try to think too much." Agnes pulled her from the vortex of self-damaging thoughts.

Sitheia blinked several times before the smiling face of the herbalist came into focus.

"Oh, I am sorry. For a moment I considered how big the world is outside our lovely village and I tried to figure out our role in it."

"And? What did you figure?" Agnes raised her left eyebrow making Sitheia laugh.

"Nothing. I am just being silly. I guess I am getting old."

They both burst into laughter at that. Finally when Agnes stopped laughing she reminded Sitheia that there was a reason why she has come here this evening instead of going home to celebrate.

"I assume that you have come to see me this evening for more than just because you missed my company." Said Agnes and she went back behind the counter and started making room on top of it so that Sitheia can unload her bag.

"I am always happy to come and visit. I always learn new things."

"Oh, if that was true maybe I should start charging you rather than paying you. So, what do you have for me tonight?"

Sitheia left her unfinished sweetroll on the stool and dropped her leather bag that was made by her mother on the countertop.

"Two silvers and 65 coppers." Sitheia demanded as she gently pulled the fresh herbs from her bag and laid them out on the countertop.

"Cheap… cheap… cheap…" Agnes commented as she inspected the many purple, red, orange and blue flowers. "Not so cheap." She said looking at two fat roots and then she smiled. The last flower had seven very small white petals. Agnes picked it carefully and inspected it from closer. "Nice, very nice and it's in perfect condition."

In an instant her smile vanished as she fixed Sitheia with her eyes.

"Sitty. You didn't go there again?" The small flowers with white petals grew only at the base of the ruined tower, a place that was off limits for everyone. "You can hurt yourself up there, you know that. You can get yourself killed."

"Don't worry, Mrs. Agnes. I am very careful. I know every rock and every stone in there. I know where it's safe to step on and where it's not."

"It's not about that. Physical danger is only one small problem out there. Those ruins have been magically sealed for thousands of years. It must have been done for a reason." Agnes put a hand on Sitheia's shoulder. "That place may hold anything from restless spirits to evil curses. It's not safe. I am saying this for your own good."

"I know that you care about me and I appreciate that. But, the tower is not dangerous for me. I don't need the Door to open. I don't care about what is inside. I just need to see the Door from time to time and be around that place. It's so beautiful I can hardly describe it. It's like the most peaceful place in the world and from there I can see the whole valley. It's breathtaking. You know, I can show it to you someday when you are not busy. That is, if you want me to."

"Thanks, but I'll have to take your word for it."

"Mrs. Agnes. I know that you need these little things. You know how rare they are."

"Sitty. I would never forgive myself if you ever got hurt while chasing these herbs. The silver myrtle is rear and very valuable plant, but it is not more valuable than your life."

Agnes saw that there was no point giving grief to Sitheia any longer, so she paid for the herbs and let the girl go. With worried expression she watched as Sitheia left her store with the half eaten sweetroll in her hand.

CHAPTER 9

The cool evening air felt good on her neck as it waved her long messy hair. Sitheia did her best not to get any of it over her sweetroll. The moon was gone making the night darker than usual. There was music and laughter coming from the Inn, the usual gathering place for the people of Sacred Pools. Sitheia doubted that even the market had as much traffic as the Inn. She noticed that tonight there were more horses than usual tied in front of the Inn.

'Probably the emissaries are still here.' She thought. If it was any other night she would be curious enough to enter the Inn and sneak into a corner from where she can hear and see everything without being noticed. Underage Cat were not allowed at the Inn after dark so she had plenty of opportunities to practice her sneaking skills. After tonight she would never have to hide inside the Inn and she will be able to enter whenever she liked. Probably it wouldn't be as fun.

But the Inn was not where she was going now, no matter how curious she was. It was her birthday and her family was waiting for her at home. She was late and she needed to hurry. They were all waiting for her and it wasn't fair to keep them waiting for no reason.

She turned away from the Inn and in short time she stood in front of her home. It was quiet. Sitheia let out a heavy breath. Have they eaten already and gone to bed? Is it that late? She didn't expected noise like at the Inn, but still, it was her birthday. She hoped to have at least a small party. She pushed the door open.

"SURPRISE!" Came from all sides.

"HAPPY BIRTHDAY! HAPPY BIRTHDAY!"

"HAPPY BIRTHDAY!"

"HAPPY BIRTHDAY! HAPPY BIRTHDAY!"

Every smiley face that meant something to her came smiling and cheering in front of her eyes. The large living room got much lighter and warmer now that her grandfather removed the curtain that was hiding the fire. There were also several candles and a lantern that her family has tried to hide behind things.

"Oh, guys. When I saw the house quiet and dark I

thought that you have all gone to bed already."

"That's why it's called a surprise, silly." Her sister chirped and laughed at the rime that become apparent to her. "He, he. Silly, Sitty. Silly, Sitty."

"Thank you all so much."

"I can never forget anything about you Sitty." A tall blond man said from behind her sister.

"John! You are here too?" Sitheia was happy to see him come to her birthday party.

"Your father invited me. I didn't want to intrude." The big man said uncertain.

"Nonsense. You are not intruding." Sitheia said smiling. Her mother looked like she wanted to disagree, but she choose to remain silent and hugged her daughter instead.

Sitheia got buried under many hands each wanting to hug her and to congratulate her. Her sister rushed in to hug her first.

"Happy birthday, Sitty." She also took advantage of the opportunity to pull her sister's ears. It is tradition after all.

Mary and George Cat hugged their daughter next.

"Happy birthday, sweetheart." Her father kissed her forehead and stepped back so her mother can have a turn.

"By the Goddess. Happy birthday, Sitty. Happy birthday. You have grown up so fast."

"Let her breathe." Her grandfather said so that he can have his turn of congratulating his niece.

"Look at you. A grown woman, where is that snotty little girl that I used to tell stories?" Peter Cat smiled hugging her. "Happy birthday, child."

"You can still tell me stories, grandpa." Sitheia smiled back.

Last to congratulate her was John. He stood there in front of her looking at his feet and handed her something wrapped in a white cloth.

"Happy birthday." He mumbled.

Sitheia took the gift without opening it and just gave him a hug. It took a few moments for John to relax in her arms. When she pulled from the hug, he pointed to the gift that he gave her.

"Your dagger is old and rusty. You struggle when you cut herbs with it. I got you a new one."

It took her no time to unwrap the gift. Inside the fabric she found a small dagger like the one that she already had. Only this one was new. She hugged John one more time making her mother twitch uncomfortably.

"Thank you." Sitheia said to John squeezing his arm in appreciation and managed to pull a smile from John in the end.

"Hello, Sitheia." A voice that Sitheia did not recognize drew her attention.

John stepped aside to reveal a small figure. Sitheia looked toward Melinda a high priestess of the Goddess. That was the same high priestess that Sitheia managed to interrupt in her prayer that morning. Sitheia hoped that Melinda was not here because of the three headed dragon incident that morning.

The priestess was a small person, a bit shorter than Sitheia and she was draped in dark red clothes from head to toes. Her face was barely visible under the hood and Sitheia noticed that the face of the woman was somehow blank.

The priestess looked to be younger than her mother and she always freaked her out because her face didn't seem to be having any expressions that you may find on a living person.

Sitheia knew that Melinda lived and worked at the temple and was rarely seen outside of it. She served the Goddess. It was an important job, so she didn't have the time to deal with matters of the mundane world. But for some strange reason she was also present here at Sitheia's birthday party.

"Happy birthday Sitheia." The voice of the priestess sounded strange, a bit guttural like the voice of someone who is not in the habit of speaking a lot.

"Thanks." Sitheia said quietly. Not sure how she should respond, she curtsied. The lips of the priestess stretched in a smile. For some reason that made Sitheia tried to brush some of the dirt from her clothes.

"It is not a common thing, a Cat coming of age." The words of the priestess were coming slow but firm making Sitheia fidget even more over her dirty clothes. "A moment that happens once in a lifetime. Two thousand years ago a bargain was made. We serve, the Lords protect and the Goddess watches over all of us so that we all keep our part of the bargain. In the eyes of the Cat people, the Lords of Perdival and the Goddess, I recognize you Sitheia."

Sitheia gulped, this was obviously more than a party visit. But, she's never heard of this and she didn't know how to respond so she remained quiet.

"In the months ahead, your value will be tested and your worth will be determined. Take this and serve well so that the bargain will be kept until she awakes."

Sitheia noticed that the priestess have lifted her right arm and a strange pendant was hanging from her palm. Her mother nudged her forward, so she took the pendant not removing her eyes from the priestess.

"Thank you," she mumbled.

Melinda did not say anything. Without looking or saying anything to anyone she just left, leaving Sitheia to watch at the closed door with an opened mouth.

"Close your mouth, Sitty, before you catch a fly." Grandpa Peter reminded her.

It was all quiet for a moment and then everyone started

to gather around her.

"Congratulations, Sitty."

"What was that?" Sitheia asked at last.

"It's our tradition, Sitty." Her father said.

"When a person comes of age, the High priestess of the Goddess formally recognizes that person as an adult." Her mother said rubbing her daughter's back.

"How come I've never seen this before? I've never even heard her speak to anyone."

"They don't speak. The priestesses."

"Ever?"

"The only time they are speaking is when they are saying the ritual words that you've just heard. Those exact same words have been spoken since the days when the bargain was made." Her grandpa said.

"How is it possible that they never speak?" Dana asked.

"They do speak. With the Goddess and they speak only with their minds." Peter Cat winked at both of them. "For mundane things, they have the acolytes to speak for them."

"You mean they can read our minds?" Dana asked scared.

"Why? Did you think of something bad?" Her father asked.

"No… I mean… I thought she sounded like a man. Is that bad?" The girl asked.

"Dana Cat, that is rude."

"But, I didn't say it. It just crossed my mind. Did I offend her?"

"Don't worry child. The priestesses of the Goddess have more important things on their mind then reading the mind of little children." Her father said.

"Don't worry about it, Dana. The priestesses are nice. They don't hold grudges over stray thoughts." Sitheia said.

"By the Goddess. How did you managed to get your clothes so dirty, again? It's like you've been rolling on the street out there like a foal."

Her mother tried to dust off some of the dirt, before she realized how her daughter might have gotten that much dirt over her clothes.

"You were at the tower again." She accused her daughter.

"Hey, let's not forget that there was a party in here." Sitheia smiled away her mother's accusation. "Don't I get some presents?"

Her mother gave her a fake stern look and smiled right after. She opened a casket that was near the wall and pulled what seemed to be a big pile of clothes.

"This is from me and your dad." She pushed everything in her daughter's hands that got overwhelmed by the stuffs and almost stumbled and dropped some of the clothes.

"Since you have a habit of climbing and going through

the forest…" Her father started.

"And that means dirty and torn clothes." Her mother cut in.

"And since now you are officially an adult…" Her father continued.

"We can't have you moving among adults looking as if you were a drifter." Her mother finished his sentence again.

"It's why we decided to give you clothes that are more difficult to tear…"

"And no one will know if they are dirty because of the color."

Sitheia always found it funny how her parents had a habit of speaking the same thing in turns, finishing each other sentences.

She put the clothes at the table in front of her and inspected her gift. It looked just like any other village clothes except that they were dark brown, not that uncommon. Sitheia felt them with her hand. John mirrored her motion by default.

"It's firm." She noticed.

"It's an armor." John said tapping it with his knuckles.

"It's made of hardened lather. It looks like any other respectable clothes, but actually it is an armor." Her mother beamed full of pride.

"You made it?" Sitheia asked incredulous.

"Your father caught the deer, just the right age and

color. It is very difficult to find and you see this fittings in here. They are made of wolf skin."

"It took quite some time to track that one. There are no wolves in this area." Her father said.

"I tanned the hides and sewed the clothes together."

"I helped, with the fat." Dana joined in.

"Yes, your sister helped as well."

Sitheia had no words. She didn't know of a better gift than this. Wearing this, she will never get scratched again. No more walking around with holes in her clothes and she didn't even need to use all of her saved money.

"Do you like it?" Her mother prompted her to say something.

"I love it. Thank you so much." Sitheia hugged everyone again.

Sitheia already was looking if she can put it on right away, but her mother stopped her.

"You can put it on tomorrow and if it needs some fitting we will sort it out then."

"All right."

Her sister Dana came in front of her with her hands behind her back.

"I have something for you as well." She said smugly. The young girl brought her two little fists and held them in midair. "Take a guess. Pick one."

"This one." Sitheia touched the one to the left.

"How did you know?" Her sister was amazed. She opened her hand and there was a single copper in it. "Happy birthday. This is a magical coin. I took it to the temple and washed it in the blessed basin. It will bring you luck."

Sitheia hugged her sister.

"Thank you. I will care it with me forever." That made the young girl to smile from ear to ear.

Sitheia and Dana helped their mother to bring food and plates to the table while George poured mead for the adults and juice made of cornel cherry for Dana. Peter filled the fireplace with wood making the whole room warm.

John felt uncomfortable staying for dinner, but Sitheia wanted him to stay and there was no discussion after that. At least he refused the alcohol and took a glass of juice. For some reason that was the first thing that Mary approved about him.

As everyone sat around the table, Sitheia looked around. They were blessed. They had this big house where they were all warm and cozy and they had this much food to feast on. The bread that her mother has baked this time was made with yeast fed with honey. She loved this bread, but her mother was making it only for special occasions. There were also two large meat pies and some potato salad, boiled corn cobs and her father had roasted a whole venison leg.

"To your health! Let you may have at least a thousand

more birthdays." Her grandpa raised his cup first and the rest joined in the cheer.

"For Sitty!"

"Happy birthday."

"Cheers!"

"Cheers!"

Sitheia took a sip from the mead and felt that she was blushing. It was sweet, but also she felt that it kind of burned a little in her throat and then her belly. She smiled and reminded herself to be careful with that.

"You are an adult now. Now you are allowed to have a drink with the adults." Her father smiled at his daughter's reaction to the alcohol.

The evening went on until most of the food was gone. They decided to take a little break chatting before they have some of the sweet birthday pie.

"Grandpa? Why don't you give me your gift now?" Sitheia asked.

"My gift, now?" The elderly man asked.

"Yes, let us hear a story."

"A story? What that has got to do with my gift?"

"Come on, grandpa. I want to hear a story." Sitheia begged.

The old man considered something for a moment and said.

"All right then. I know a story that may be interesting

to hear. It was late autumn. The weather was getting cold and wet already. The trails were wet and slippery. The harvest that year was good, but my friend Victor and I, we thought that it would be good for us if might bag some last moment game to make the winter easier and more fun.

So, the two of us set out hours before dawn. We walked for a long time. We circled around the mountain and we got to a cave. It stank like something awful. We both knew that we hit the vain.

We were not sure what was inside, but by the smell, we guessed that it might be anything from a bear to a wyvern. Since wyverns rarely come in these parts and they prefer open ground rather than caves except when they are about to nest, we thought that it was definitely a bear. We were right, but obviously the bear that was preparing for the winter sleep, wasn't there yet. It was still too early for her to go to sleep.

And just as we smelled her, so did she smelled us. Like someone brought her dinner right to her home. Think of that. If someone brought you your dinner to your house, wouldn't that make life a lot easier? Not to have to hunt and harvest and cook."

"Focus, dad." George prompted the old man to stay on his story.

"Right, where was I? Yes, the bear. She came out rather faster than we expected. In fact, I have never seen a beast moving that fast. Before we had time to raise our spear or draw our swords she swinged her paw at poor Victor throwing him in a tree.

I am not proud of myself. But, when she came after me I ducked and run for it dropping my spear. I knew that she was right behind me and that I cannot outrun her. I thought passed through my mind about climbing a tree. But, before I had the time to make any stupid decisions, I tripped. I swear to the Goddess I did. I fell right on my nose.

The bear was running so fast that she couldn't stop her run as fast. So she passed over me. I turned as I lay there with bloody face. I got my bow off my shoulder and knocked an arrow. I have been hunting all my life, just as my father has done before me and his father before and as George here is doing now. Many times I have used arrows to catch a beast, but my life never has depended on my archery skill as it did that day. I aimed and released the arrow. And after that I released a dozen more, one after the other as fast as I could.

I heard thump. When I lifted my head I saw the bear was not moving and my arrows were sticking from all sides. I got up and went to see if Victor was still alive. He was and I thank the Goddess that he was or I wouldn't be here now. As I was bending over him to see how serious he was injured, he whispered "Look out."

I turned and I heard her before I saw her. The angry bear running with all the arrows I already put in her still stuck in her flash. I was out of my mind already. I grabbed one of the spears that we dropped on the ground and aimed it at the bear, digging its but into the ground.

And that's it. The bear was dead, my friend had a broken arm and we had to return to the village to bring more people and horses with a cart to be able to bring the bear. The village celebrated us. We had plenty of delicious meat and that fur that my bed is covered with came from that bear."

As he finished everyone was quiet for a while.

"Wait, grandpa. What are you talking about? I thought you were going to tell us a story." Sitheia protested.

"I just did."

"Not that story. We have all heard the story about how you killed the bear a hundred times."

"Well what kind of story do you want? You said you wanted a story about my gift? That is the only story about my gift that I remember that is worth telling."

"What are you talking about? What gift?" Sitheia was totally lost.

Her grandpa smiled at her. He stood from his chair telling her:

"You wait here." And he climbed downstairs where their beds were.

"What is going on?" Sitheia looked for an answer from her parents.

"You'll have to wait and see for yourself." Her father said with a smile, while her mother had a sour expression on her face which confused Sitheia even more.

She listened intently as her grandfather climbed the stairs back. He held something in his hands, a bow.

"Here it is. This is my old bow. I haven't been using it for a long time, but I've been restoring it for the last two months. Your John here has been helping me with it. So, I think that it can still work…"

He wasn't able to finish because Sitheia gave him a strong hug that nearly knocked him off his feet.

"Thank you. Thank you. Thank you so much."

"Wait a minute." Her mother interfered. "That is very kind of you Peter. But, I don't think that a bow is an appropriate gift for a girl."

"Why not?" Sitheia asked.

"Because now that you are an adult, you need to start thinking about how you will be bringing value to Sacred Pools and hope to be picked to work at the castle."

"Well, I can be a hunter. Our family has been hunting for generations, I will continue the tradition."

"The men in the family have been hunting for generations, not the women. You have your way with words. Maybe you can be a trader. You can start selling our furs and hides and then maybe the Lords will take you to trade for them."

"But, I enjoy walking through the forest. Your gift, the armor says that you understand that." Sitheia was determined not to give up on her freedom.

"Then you can be a herbalist like Agnes. She has thought you a lot about herbs. You can learn how to brew potions."

"Mary, honey. Perhaps we can discuss how she will be bringing value tomorrow. As for the bow, there is no harm in having it. She moves around the woods a lot and it is good to have something more to defend herself than that tiny little dagger."

Mary agreed to let go of the subject at least for now. There was no reason to take the joy out of the party with the serious discussions that will happen anyway the next day. She gave her daughter a small smile that Sitheia took as resigning.

"Thank you." She said again to everyone as she took the bow in her hands. She twitched her nose.

It had a strong smell of oils. She wanted to try it out right away, but she knew that she will have to leave that for the next day as well, just like her new clothes. Putting the bow on top of the pile that was her new clothes and her new dagger, Sitheia focused on what was her intention from the beginning of the conversation.

"Now, tell us a story."

"Another one?" Her grandpa was shocked. "I just told you one. Didn't you like that one? I wouldn't be alive if it wasn't for that story."

"No, the story was nice... but... I was hoping for one of the other ones."

"What other ones?" Grandpa Peter pretended not to understand what stories his niece was asking for.

"You know. The other ones. The ones about the past."

"Ooo. You want one of those stories." He acted to be just realizing what she is asking for. "You want to know about the times before we came here. You want to know about the time when the deal was made with Lord Perdival."

"Yes, I want to know about the wars." Sitheia couldn't wait.

"What wars? Our people have never been in a war." Her grandpa protested. "The Cat people are not warlike. We create, we shape things, and we bring value. That is our way of life. It always has been."

"But, what about the war that was going on before Lord Perdival found us?" Sitheia asked.

"Well, that was not our war. Our people have been caught in the middle of it, but we didn't start it and we sure didn't fight it. Our forefathers have done everything they could to keep us away from it. That is why are people have survived for so long, for more than two thousand years. It is not a small feat to achieve."

"Tell it from the beginning." Sitheia was pushing things the way she wanted.

"Very well then. Here is how it was:

"It was more than two thousand years ago, when there was chaos across the land. The Lords of various holds have been squabbling and fighting among themselves. One day they are allies, the next day they are at each other's throats. While at the same time old enemies have been forging unusual alliances against other Lords.

They've been fighting so much amongst themselves that there wasn't even a thought toward the unity that exists today, with one ruler over the entire land. It was only after the appearance of orcish invaders from the south that the Lords started to join forces, but that was several hundred years later.

Now, most of the people of the Northern Star Kingdom believe that the war was all about greedy Lords looking to grab some of their neighbor's land. But we, the Cat people, we know the secret. In those chaotic times demons and evil spirits form other worlds manipulated the minds of the Lords so that they would serve their twisted goals without even knowing. To everyone else those demons and evil spirits looked exactly like any other people, but we knew the true. Our blood was blessed so that we can see them and recognize them no matter how they hide their ugly faces.

But, we were not the only one who had an advantage. The demons, they were also able to recognize us. It has been passed down through the generations that those demons were able to smell our blood from miles away.

To eliminate the only threat that stood in the way of total domination over the entire world, the demons pulled on their strings. They whispered in the ears of the Lords corrupting their minds with each word pushing them to fight with other Lords. And the chosen battlegrounds just happen to be the land where our ancestors lived. It was so long time ago that the name that our ancestors used to call themselves have been lost and no one remembers it.

We are not warlike people, we never were. Caught between two raging armies controlled by those who wanted us extinct, our people had no choice but to gather what possessions they could carry with them and try to avoid the armies."

"Why they didn't try to fight back?" Sitheia asked.

"There is a reason why our people are not warlike. It is like the gods don't want us to be."

"The gods?"

"Yes. We have hunters, you know that. Your father is a hunter. I was a hunter and so was my father. It is very likely that our line of hunters goes back from the times that I am telling you about."

"What that has got to do with it?"

"Well, for one thing. It means that they had weapons. We have bows and spears, sometimes we use short swords and at the very least we have knives and daggers. Magic is not that uncommon among our people, but they all turn to be either priests or they go to work in the castle. My point is that they, our people were armed. And from my story about the bear you can tell that we are not cowards."

"So what was the problem?" Sitheia pushed for more information.

"For some reason their weapons didn't work as they should."

"What do you mean the weapons didn't work? There is nothing to work in them. You just stab or hack at someone."

"Well, if you let me tell the story instead off interrupting me all the time you can learn that they were unable to stab or hack or shoot someone with an arrow."

"How… sorry, I won't interrupt you again. Go on."

"I believe myself that we have been cursed. When a Cat person tries to do harm to another person, they fail. You swing a sword at someone and the blade stops in midair. Like there is an invisible hand that stops the blade from reaching its target. Everyone among our ancestors who carried weapons and tried to fight back were astonished to find that they can't hurt their opponents and they all died being unable to defend themselves. That is why the rest decided to flee and they tried to hide.

As they ran trying to save their skins, demons in the form of half wolf half man started attacking them. Funny thing about these beasts is that our ancestors' weapons worked on them partially. They were able to stab them or shoot them and the blades were able to pierce the skin of the monsters, but they didn't die. It would only slow them down for a short time and then they would be on their feet again biting and growling as nothing has even scratched them. The wolf-men picked the animals from the small heard that our people had, eating them one at a time until none were left.

Our people had to fend off the monsters' attacks that never stopped and now they were facing the possibility of starving to death. In that desperate hour when are people were at the verge of extinction, they came out of nowhere. Our saviors.

At the head of his army, Lord Perdival came from the sky flying on his winged horse. Every warrior from his army carried those special shiny blades, swords coated with silver. The wolves fell under the silver blades and those that did not, fled. When the battle was over the noble warriors came to the villagers with healers to tend to the wounded. The elder who was leading our ancestors fell on his knees before Lord Perdival and begged him to take our people under his protection, promising that in return our people will serve him as long as they protect us.

On that faithful day a sacred contract was struck, with blood and magic. You heard some of it from priestess Melinda. Lord Perdival brought our people to his land and gave them permission to build settlements. Two villages were built, our village where we produce food and clothes. The other village was Silville where the villagers mine silver that the Lords of Perdival use to make the swords that kill demons.

Lord Perdival named our people Cat to hide their identity from the demons that still had the ears of the Lords and could send more armies after us. We took the Goddess that was worshipped by Lord Perdival's people as our own and she has been generous.

For two thousand years the Lords of Perdival have kept their side of the bargain and they have protected whether by fighting monsters, bandits or helping us live through harsh winters. We also kept our side of the bargain and served however we could. We give large part of what we produce to them, but we always keep enough so that we may live in comfort.

Occasionally, emissaries from the castle would come and identify people with skills or abilities that can be of more use if they were working at the castle than in the village. People from the village have served at the castle doing everything from being cooks, chambermaids, builders, taking care of the stables, forging and repairing their weapons and armor or as traders or scribes.

Those that serve one of the Lords who do the trading for the castle, travel with them and we have seen them on occasion passing through the village with carts of goods. When I was only a boy I remember there was a very smart girl who was taken to serve a Perdival's ambassador in Starcross City and she lived there her entire life."

"And what about grandma?" Sitheia asked startling everyone.

Peter's eyes got unfocused for a moment as if he was remembering Faith Cat, his wife and Sitheia's grandmother. Then he smiled and looked at Sitheia.

"It is a great honor for a family if they are able to help maintain the sacred contract with the Lords of Perdival. It was less than a year before you were born. Faith started having… visions that short time after would come true. With the visions came headaches. As more visions came, the stronger the headaches got.

Lord Gavin came, he did some kind of spell on Faith and the pain stopped, but he said that it will come back. Lord Gavin said that Faith being in the castle would benefit everyone by them being able to react faster to her visions and they will help her lessen the burden of the headaches."

"I am sorry I asked, it must be painful talking about that." Sitheia said, placing a hand over her grandpa's.

"I miss her every day. I thought that we will grow old together. But, I am proud and very happy for her. As I said, it is a great honor for a member of a family to be picked to serve at the castle."

Later that night when Sitheia laid in her bed with her eyes opened her thought returned to the Alchemist's Hut and her meeting with Lord Gavin. For some reason she forgot to mention it to her family, probably because she was distracted with the celebration. At least that is what Sitheia told herself.

What if they really picked her to go and work at the castle? Everyone talked about that being a great honor, but she didn't really cared that much about honor. She didn't want to maybe never see her family again.

A little voice inside her head protested "But, why would they pick her? What did she have to offer them? She knew how to find herbs, but didn't know what to do with them. Her mother had taught her how to tan leather, but she didn't enjoy doing that. Sitheia considered that she might actually be good at hunting, but since she has never used a bow before, she couldn't tell if she was any good or not.

She could add and subtract and knew how to sell, but she had no patience to deal with customers, at least not with the customers that were buying from her parents. Sitheia also was able to write, but she always rushed to get it done quickly, so her writing ended up looking like as if a chicken has dipped her feet in the ink and walked over the paper."

"There is nothing special about me. I got nothing that they may want from me." She whispered for herself.

There was a slight problem with her logic. Sitheia knew that now that she was an adult, her family, the villagers and the Lords of Perdival will be expecting for her to contribute some kind of value.

As much as it was an honor for a person to be picked to serve, it was considered a disgrace to be unable to provide any value neither for the village nor for your family. Sitheia didn't want to disgrace her family or be a burden for them. But she also didn't want to never see them again.

Remembering the words of her grandpa she came to the conclusion that if she was a hunter, she would not be forced to stay inside the castle. Or she may be a trader and she will be able to see her family when she will be passing through the village if she was traveling with a caravan.

"Hunting or trading." She whispered again.

One of those two trades is what she needed to learn how to be better at. With those thoughts in mind Sitheia finally closed her eyes.

CHAPTER 10

The next day Sitheia found herself cornered by her parents during breakfast. She knew that this conversation was inevitable, but until this moment the whole adult thing didn't seem all that real.

"So, have you given a thought about how you are going to produce value? Is there something that pulls your curiosity more than anything else?" George asked.

For a second Sitheia got confused by the formulation of that question, because the first thing that popped in her mind was the image of her most treasured friend, The Door. But, immediately it become clear to her that her parents wouldn't be all that happy about hearing that an old ruin is their daughter's best friend. Sitheia almost dropped her piece of bread with jam made of plums.

It just dawned on her that if she was to be picked to go and live in the castle she would also have to abandon The Door. For some reason the thought of being away from her tower seemed unbearable. She felt tightening in her chest as if something heavy was pressing on her. Sitheia managed to hide her thoughts by answering her father.

"Actually, I have. You were right last night." She turned toward her mother. "I am very good at finding herbs. And Mrs. Agnes have always been telling me that I should learn how to make use of the herbs that I am bringing to her and brewed them into potions. I thought that I may ask her to teach me. What do you think?"

"Healing is a very noble trade, my dear. That is a very good choice." Her mother said giving her daughter a one armed hug.

"Yes, and I will be able to hunt while I am picking the herbs so I will be doing two trades simultaneously." Agreed Sitheia, but her mother crossed her eyebrows in an instant.

"Most certainly not. It is one thing for a little girl to be playing with things like that. But, a grown woman to be hunting? That is not a profession suitable for a female. Why don't you learn how to cook? The bakery certainly can use the help or the Inn. Or you can learn how to tan the hides of the animals that the hunters are bringing like I am doing."

"Mom, I don't want to take care of the kills of other hunters. I want to catch the animals by myself. And as far as cooking goes I know what is really important. You take the animal that you have killed, you'll first need to skin it and remove the insides. You'll sharpen a piece of wood and spit roast the animal over the fire until it is dark enough so you can tell that it is cooked."

Mary Cat was looking at her daughter with wide open eyes as Sitheia was explaining her way of cooking, not being able to close her stunned mouth.

"Why don't we leave the hunting for later and concentrate on the alchemy for start, unless you have some other profession on your mind?" George diverted the conversation seeing that it wasn't moving in a desirable direction.

"Well, I thought that I may also learn trading. You know, to learn how to be a merchant." Sitheia said looking from one parent to the other uncertain of what their thinking was. "I was thinking that I may help in the leatherworker shop and maybe at the Inn or with the blacksmith. I thought that as a merchant it would be good for me to learn how to trade different types of products. I don't know what I am going to be good at so I was thinking that by trying these things one of them will stand out as the better choice for a real profession."

"I understand. Very smart." Her father said making

Sitheia smile.

"Yes, and the professions that you have picked are things that may be of use to the castle as well." Her mother smiled at Sitheia too. "If you can only stop worrying us with the talks about you being a hunter and I couldn't be happier."

"We all do what we feel that we must. That is what the Goddess teaches us. Right?" Sitheia said more for herself but her parents heard it too, so she added. "Don't worry. I am not going to become a priestess."

"Why not, that is also a very noble profession?" Her mother said with a smile and Sitheia couldn't tell if she was teasing her or she was serious.

***

For years Sitheia has been gathering herbs and selling them to Agnes. During that time, on occasions the herbalist has been giving her pointers about some of the properties that various plants possessed. Mostly that information has been about what certain plant is used for and how to approach the extraction of certain herbs that needed a little more delicate handling. All of those lessons have been about plants that Sitheia has brought for selling or about plants that Agnes wanted Sitheia to find for her. But, asking the herbalist to accept her as an apprentice was somehow different and the prospect of it made Sitheia a little nervous.

Immediately after her conversation with her parents Sitheia planned to go and gather some herbs and then to visit Agnes and ask if she would take her as an apprentice. The secret plan behind that was to use the opportunity to practice some hunting since she was already in the woods. Unfortunately, her mother suspected that going into the woods would just give her daughter a chance to play with that silly bow that she got for her birthday.

A thought crossed Sitheia's mind that she can point out that now she was an adult and that it was her decision, but she chased the thought from her head. She didn't agree with her mother's point of view, but she also knew that her mother had her best interests at heart and there was no point in starting a quarrel with her over this. She knew that in the end she will be out there hunting as much as she liked. It didn't matter to her whether it was going to be today or tomorrow.

She started by helping in the leatherwork and tannery shop that her parents owned. It was a small two room building that was right next to their house. You can say that the shop was part of the house, because they were under the same roof and they were also sharing a wall. But, the shop had a separate front and back entrance.

The backroom of the shop was partially a storage area and partially a place where the manufacturing of the leather occurred. The backyard was where the skins were stretched for drying and tanning. The front room of the shop was where the tanned hides were displayed for sale along with some products made of leather such as belts, clothes, bags and backpacks and all other sorts of things that were made of leather that could find use in a household.

Sitheia was not enthusiastic about working with hides and furs, but it turned out that people needed them for all sorts of things. They were buying them as material for making clothes and also as covers for beds, floors and walls. Sitheia discovered that the more she talked to the customer while she was trying to sell them something, the more they bought. Very often it happened for them to go home buying a lot more than they needed. While Sitheia was very happy with those transactions, her parents weren't. Almost every time, the people would come back with the extra products to return them saying: that they have no idea why they even bought so much.

"It is very good that you are able to sell so many products, but it is not our goal to trick our neighbors into buying things that they don't need." Probably both her parents have said this to her at least several times.

Thankfully, in the backyard her father had built for her a target made of wood and straw, where she can practice archery. Frustrated by the futility of the trade that she was supposed to learn, Sitheia took it as an inspiration for practicing archery.

She wasn't that bad considering that in her entire life she has been shooting arrows only when she was a kid and from a small bow that was more a toy than a real weapon. Even though after her first practice session she hasn't gotten anywhere near the center of the target, at least she felt that some of her frustration was left on the target.

Whenever Sitheia got frustrated with her trading restrictions she went in the back to shoot some arrows. At last Sitheia raised her hands from trading at her parents store and asked Mr. Olaf from the Inn if he needed help. She found it interesting that for some reason no one argued if she sold more mead or ale. Even the Prince showed up one time and she almost tripped over her own feet, but she managed not to make a mess.

As far as Alchemy as a trade went, Mrs. Agnes was more than happy to start teaching her how to brew potions. But, she insisted that Sitheia first needed to understand how the herbs and minerals interacted with each other when exposed to different elements. Only then she will start to actually brew potions, otherwise she would just be repeating the motions without having any idea what or why things were happening.

This teaching approach helped very much with Sitheia's archery practice.

Sitheia spent the next couple of weeks doing her best to be useful to her family. Sitheia was a girl of action. She needed to do things, to feel that something was happening as a result of what she was doing. Memorizing explanations about how she would be doing those things was eating her from the inside.

After two weeks spent between learning about plants and potions and then selling ale and food to the people that visited the Inn, Sitheia was very close to replace the target in the backyard for some of her customers.

With every day passing she was getting more and more irritable. She was losing patience fast with the customers. The isolated nature of the village meant that the only customers were the people of Sacred Pools and the social norms dictated not to take advantage of the trusting nature of your neighbors.

The slow progress with alchemy wasn't helping either. After a month, all she has learned was two healing methods. One salve that was used as a poultice over small surface wounds, more like scratches. The other was a concoction that needed to be taken with tea three times a day, it was a cough medicine. She was certain that Mrs. Agnes believed that she was teaching her a lot more, but these were the only things of value Sitheia was able to find in her teachings.

She was able to see John occasionally when he would visit her at the Inn, but even he constantly reminded her that she needs to be patient. He also reminded her on a daily basis that she can't start shooting arrows at her countrymen just because they were pissing her off. Sitheia saw the Prince visiting the Inn on one of his inspections. Only she was so frustrated that she just kept herself out of sight in order to avoid an incident.

The worst part about the time that she has spent working was that she hasn't been to visit the Door for a whole month. Every day she wanted to just drop everything that she was doing and to just go to the tower. Every day the pull was getting stronger, she even saw the tower in almost every dream that she had.

Thanks to the general feeling of frustration with the development of her chosen professions, her archery was getting much better. During this period, the only times that she got close to being happy was while she was shooting arrows.

Sitheia discovered that at the moment before she released the arrow, her focus was so strong that she felt calmer than she has ever felt in her entire life. After that discovery, Sitheia made sure that she practices as often as she could get away with. She half suspected that the feeling of calm was the prime reason for her interest in archery.

One afternoon after a particularly irritating day, John came over to see how Sitheia was doing. He found her in the backyard making a pincushion out of the target.

"You are getting really good at archery." He said before entering the yard.

"I am having a lot of motivation to practice." She smiled at him. Seeing John always made her feel better. "It was either to shoot arrows at the target or at the customers. The target won this time."

As John got closer he was able to see that there was at least a dozen arrows stuck close to the center of the target and there were many more around the center.

"I see that you have a lot of arrows." John pointed at the bucket full of arrows that was right next to her leg.

"Making arrows is another way for me to save the lives of my fellow villagers." Sitheia smiled.

She took a deep breath and held it. She aimed, focusing on the center of the target blurring the world around her. This was the moment that made the practice of archery so tempting. She felt like her whole body was one with that dot in the center of the target. Her mind got cleared of everything else, of all the tension that has built up inside her. Her body followed her mind and relaxed as well. In one moment, she released the breath and the arrow and watched it fly and hit the center.

John cheered her by clapping his hands.

"Bravo!"

Sitheia made a mock curtsying with the bow in one hand and a new arrow in the other.

"If you have come to make me feel better," Sitheia started looking at his boyish grin, "than you have succeeded."

Sitheia left the bow next to the bucket with arrows, pulled two apples from her bag and throw one at John who caught it midair. They sat on the porch and ate quietly.

"I haven't seen you in a while." Sitheia noted.

"I am sorry. I should have come by sooner. It's just that I've been helping the masons. We are expanding the lumber mill by the river so that they can do more work and I've been helping there from dawn 'till dusk."

Sitheia touched his arm above the elbow. John has always been strong and had large muscles, but now his biceps felt much firmer than before and maybe a little tensed.

"You are not pushing yourself too hard, are you?"

"It's hard." He admitted. "But, I am helping and at least I am providing value."

"John. You don't have to prove anything to anyone." Sitheia was worried about him. "You need to think of what is good for you. Don't let them take advantage of you."

He watched his half eaten apple for a while before answering with a strained smile.

"I assume that you are here destroying that target because you are following your own advice."

"I didn't say that I was smart." She said bitterly. "But, you are right. I wanted to try to become a merchant. So I tried. And I realized that in our village there is no one that I can actually sell anything without risking a socially awkward moment. This is why I am done trying to be a merchant. I tried to study alchemy, but all that I have learned in all this time is how to make a cough medicine and how to bandage scratches and tiny cuts."

"That is not a small thing. I mean people do cough occasionally. Ahem, ahem." John teased her by pretending that he was coughing which made her punch his shoulder.

John succeeded in making her feel a little better, but he could do nothing about her real problem. It has been way too long since the last time she has been to see the Door. She missed it bad. It started happening rather often for her to just stand in front of her house and stare over the roofs at the tower not paying attention to anything that was happening around her.

"You know. If you need that bad to relax, than maybe you should go swimming." John suggested.

"Aw no. I don't think so. As much as I love the outcome of the purification ritual, I so hate everything else about it. Also, the last time we went to the temple I am almost certain that I made a problem for Katherine. I doubt that she will be glad to see me again."

"I didn't say to go to the temple. I said that you should go to swim." John clarified.

"Then, where am I to go to swim. Am I to go and swim in the river like the small children?" She looked at John, not sure of where he was going with this. John seemed a little uncomfortable, but she was looking at him expecting an answer.

"I have discovered a secret place." He almost whispered.

"A secret place?" Sitheia looked at him with disbelief.

"Yes. Nobody knows about it, I think. If you follow where the river is flowing, you will see that it is going behind the temple, afterward there is a small waterfall where the water gathers in something like a pool before it spills out and continues until it joins the sea. That pool is deep enough that you can swim in it. The place is totally secluded, so there is no way that anyone can find it by accident."

"How did you found it?" Sitheia asked looking suspiciously at him.

"I can't tell you. And please don't pressure me, because I'll give in and I'll tell you even though I swore that I won't tell anyone."

"OK. I won't ask." Sitheia was happy that John has grown so much as a person that he was having a secret, although she was not exhilarated that he was keeping that secret from her. "Fine, let's go together tonight. We can both use some relaxation."

"Yea… That is not a very good idea." He said. "You are used to sneaking around the guards, but for me that would be a little difficult."

"Curses." Sitheia said. "It's not like I am hauling rocks

all day. Why do I feel like I am caring the whole world on my shoulders?"

"Because you are doing something that you hate." John said.

"I didn't think that I hate trading. I actually thought that I like making potions and stuffs like that." Sitheia answered wondering where things got out of hand.

"How many potions have you made so far?"

"None."

"That means that you do like the idea of making potions, it's only that you are not actually making potions." John said.

"What?"

"Sitty. I know you for a while. And in this time, I have never seen you sitting in a spot doing something that does not require action. I have never seen you knit or sew or do anything that requires for you to sit still."

"What are you saying?"

"I am saying that you have no patience for endless studying without actually doing the thing that you are studying. You learn by doing things, not by repeating instructions from a lesson." He said and Sitheia thought that he might be right. Whenever she was told to memorize something, she felt like she was wasting time. She preferred to do the thing, rather than learn about it.

"I think that you might be right." Sitheia admitted. "I

guess the same applies to trading as well. I have no patience for the customers because I am not allowed to sell them anything that might be viewed as taking advantage of them."

"Sure." He smiled at her.

"Thank you for telling me about this secret pool. I can definitely use some relaxation." Sitheia smiled at him. "And thank you for being so smart."

"You are welcome."

CHAPTER 11

John was right. Sitheia was used to sneaking around, moving in the shadows and generally avoiding the guards. She never avoided them because she was up to no good. She did it as a reflex. The reason for that was because it was always easier and more private not to be seen at all, than to have to explain where and why you are going at this hour. Sacred Pools didn't have a curfew, but it was discouraged moving around the village during the night. Even though no one has ever mentioned why, 'Has anyone even asked why?' a thought crossed Sitheia's mind.

For Sitheia, who was an expert at moving through the shadows as if she was invisible most rules about movement through the village did not applied. She moved softly and without making a sound. She had a rather small figure so it was easy for her to fit in every shadow. It was easy for her to hide behind the corner of a building, behind a fence, or inside the wheat field.

Sitheia crossed the entire village without being noticed. She spotted two patrols and honestly she pitied them. They looked like they were truly bored. Sitheia felt sympathy for them. In Sacred Pools nothing bad ever happened. The only reason why they needed guards was so that they could prevent people from moving through the village during the night and accidentally hurting themselves. It was a boring job, like most jobs in Sacred Pools. Because of that Sitheia could easily relate to them.

The night has fallen completely with the bright moon as the only thing that can reveal her presence on the streets. She passed the temple and was already out of Sacred Pools. According to the directions that she received from John, she should be going around the temple following the streaming of the river.

The path that she was following was an old dirt path that led from the village to the sea and it hasn't been used for so many years that wilderness have reclaimed most of it. Sitheia was caring a makeshift torch with her, just in case. But, there was no need to light up the torch. The moon gave all the light that she needed.

The cold breeze waved her long messy hair that she

never bothered to comb. Sitheia stopped herself in her tracks. She was outside the village, at night. If instead of going to this "Secret pool", she turns around, then she will be able to go and see the tower and the Door. The problem was that the tower stood on literally the other side of Sacred Pools. And as much as Sitheia liked to complain about how small Sacred Pools was, it would take most of the night for her to get to the tower.

There was a fork in the road that turned to the right and was barely visible because it went around some large bushes from the right side, while the left was open to the valley. Sitheia had no problem with heights but just in case she reminded herself to be careful.

She was likely getting closer because she was already hearing the water from the waterfall. John told her that there are two waterfalls. The larger one that she is probably listening is the one that drops from where she was right now to the lower level that took the river to the sea. John also warned her to stay away from this one.

Following her path she could no longer glimpse even a small part from the village. Her orientation abilities were only able to tell her that she was now on the other side of the temple. After a short walk she heard the other waterfall. This one was smaller and it seemed like it was coming out of the mountain. Sitheia could see that the large area that was opening in front of her was actually a small lake that was like a pocket for the water to gather before it spilled out into the other waterfall and joins the river. She could notice that the pool had a wall made of stones like a dam that was keeping the pool separated from the river. This pool was made on purpose and it was probably made years ago.

"Hundreds of years ago." A familiar female voice corrected her.

Sitheia looked from where the voice was coming. Surrounded by the water, illuminated only by the light of the moon, a pale female figure approached skillfully. With several clean strokes she got close enough that she could stand up. Sitheia recognized the face of Katherine, the acolyte from the temple. As the woman was getting closer to her the water from the pool was getting more and more shallow. Soon Sitheia was able to see so many pleasant parts of Katherine that she was not familiar with.

"Have you come to see me naked?" Katherine's voice sounded louder in the quiet night. She scooped water with both of her hands and poured it slowly over her breasts for Sitheia's benefit. "I get it. It's only fair. After all I have seen you naked so many times over the years."

Sitheia caught herself staring at Katherine.

"What? No. I had no idea that you would be here. I thought that nobody knew about this place." Sitheia said reverting her gaze which made Katherine chuckle.

"Why do you look away? I can tell that you like what you see." Katherine teased.

"Stay out of my head." Sitheia said. She was blushing from embarrassment, but she did have the courage to look back at Katherine. Although, she made sure that she was looking at her face.

"All right, I am sorry. I am making you uncomfortable. You came here to relax and I am making things difficult for you." Katherine pulled back into the deeper water so that she was visible only from her shoulders up. "Come on. Drop your pants and get in. The water feels great."

Sitheia hesitated a bit. She wanted to get in the water, but Katherine was making fun of her while she was fully dressed, what would it be like when she gets naked in front of her.

"For one thing, I have been seeing you naked for years. I have been touching you for years. By now, you should be used to it."

"Well, I am not. And you know, it's kind of irritating when you are having one sided conversation with my thoughts."

"I can't help you about that. It's part of me and even if I wanted, I can't turn it off."

"I know."

"OK. Let me make you a promise. If at any point, I feel that you are uncomfortable and you want me to stop teasing you and playing with you, I'll stop. I swear before the Goddess."

"I am uncomfortable now." Sitheia pointed, but she started untying the straps from her armor.

"Yes you are. But, you don't want me to stop." Katherine smiled provocatively.

With face red as a tomato, Sitheia undressed in silence. She left her armor neatly arranged on a rock. She was aware that Katherine's eyes were following her every move, but Katherine wasn't wrong. Sitheia was feeling attraction toward Katherine that she couldn't explain. It was weird and she had no idea why, but it felt so good when she was watching the acolyte swim on her back so that she can have a better view.

Sitheia felt an intense hunger, a strange emptiness inside her that this woman in front of her was able to fill. She felt saliva gathering in her mouth and a desire to bite into that flesh that was illuminated by the moon started to build up inside her.

Katherine sensing her thoughts stopped teasing, she watched as Sitheia was eating her with her eyes and shivered from the raw emotions that she felt emanating from Sitheia. She waiting for Sitheia to make a move, to come and get her.

Sitheia stood still for a while aware that her body is illuminated by the moon. Looking down at herself, she noticed that the moon was giving her a silver almost ghostlike color. Her hungry eyes found similar hunger replicated in the eyes of Katherine.

"You look different in the moonlight." Katherine made a comment. It was not a critic or teasing, it was just an observation.

"Better?" Sitheia returned the teasing to which Katherine only nodded several times unable to speak.

Not knowing how deep the water is, Sitheia slowly lowered herself in the pool. She expected that the water is going to be cold just like the river was, but it wasn't. It was lukewarm and it was gently tingling.

As soon as she entered the deeper water, Katherine got close to her like a shark coming to grab her prey.

"Why does it tingle?" Sitheia asked as she and Katherine were swimming in place facing each other.

Katherine pulled them both a little closer to the shore where they could touch the bottom with their feet.

"The water that is filling this pool comes from the inside of the mountain. It's connected with the pools inside the temple." She said touching Sitheia's arm and gently gliding her fingers from her elbow to her shoulder. "This water is heavy with healing magic. Don't you feel your body relaxing?"

Sitheia tried to withdraw inside her body and sense how she was feeling. True, most of her body was relaxing faster than if she was swimming in any other pool with ordinary water. But, what she felt for Katherine almost counteracted the effects from the enchanted water.

"So, you kind of want me, ha?" Katherine said directly without any beating around the bush and she moved closer to Sitheia.

Sitheia wasn't sure how to answer that. In fact she didn't feel like she was capable of uttering a single word. Yes, she wanted her, even though she has never wanted a girl in this way. She had this feeling before, once.

The hunger was unbearable. It felt like a tightening in her chest. Sitheia felt like she was starving and if she doesn't eat, she was going to die. Yes, she wanted her.

She moved instinctively without making conscious decisions.

"What are you thinking? I can't read you." Katherine whispered too excited to speak out loud.

Sitheia touched Katherine's face feeling the acolyte shudder under her touch. With the tips of her fingers Sitheia traced a line across her face, brushing the sticky wet hair aside ending with a finger teasing her lower lip. She got her lips so close to Katherine's that they were exchanging each other's breath.

Katherine moved closer so she can taste Sitheia's lips and missed. Sitheia pulled back just a little and pulled her lips in a soft but teasing smile.

An image of the Door flashed before her eyes and Sitheia remembered the last time that she felt like this. She knew what she was supposed to do.

She flicked her tongue so that it passed over Katherine's lower lips. Both women were breathing fast and uneven and the hunger growing in Sitheia was radiating like an aura.

"What are you doing to me?" Katherine whispered.

"You are mine." Sitheia whispered in Katherine's half open mouth.

"I am yours." Katherine accepted.

Sitheia moved forward connecting their lips. At first their lips were barely touching, but then driven by hunger and desire Sitheia pressed harder as if she was literally trying to eat her. Their lips were burning hot and they were both feeling tingling in their bodies that had nothing to do with the enchanted water. It was magical. The kiss went on for several heartbeats and it was over.

Sitheia slowly backed away. She was not feeling the hunger anymore. She was full. Looking into Katherine's eyes there was no longer excitement or desire in them, instead there was fear.

Sitheia remembered well the last time that she felt this way. It was the first time she met John. There was no more attraction toward Katherine. What she was feeling now was different. She felt a connection.

"What did you do to me?" Katherine asked with panic palpable in her voice.

Sitheia swallowed her saliva. She felt strange having to say it out loud, but there was no doubt about it. She was feeling now just like she felt when it happened with John.

"You are mine." She whispered, her words sounding hollow like they were coming from a great distance.

"No!" Katherine almost screamed swimming away from her as if she was trying to run away from her.

Sitheia didn't try to stop her. She wasn't sure if Katherine understood what just happened, she had a vague picture of what happened herself. But, what happened between them felt so natural. Sitheia had no idea how it happened, but she had no doubt about it. Just like when she was talking about John, it was the same now for Katherine.

'Katherine is mine' She thought. It was impossible to think of her in a different way.

"Hey! Who's there?!" A strong male voice brought her back to reality.

She turned and saw Katherine's ankle disappearing in the forest leading toward the temple.

Remembering that she was naked, Sitheia made sure that she was deep enough when the owner of the voice appeared. She blushed, a reflex reaction whenever she would see an emissary. It was the Prince and unlike her, he was fully dressed in a metal shiny armor completely different than his usual elegant outfit.

The armor that the Prince was wearing was shining in the moonlight looking suitable for a prince. He was even caring a red cape on his shoulders.

Sitheia felt stunned by the appearance of the Prince, but she feared that if she was discovered then she'll be in trouble. Her eyes darted to where she left her own armor.

The rock was entirely hidden by the cover of darkness and unless the Prince had a torch and she couldn't see any torches. There was just no way that he could find it.

Without too much thinking she took a breath and dived deep underwater hoping that she can hold her breath long enough for the Prince to go away. While underwater she swam toward a branch that was hanging low over the water. Once she was certain that the Prince can't see her, she slowly lifted her head above the surface to get some air.

The branch was hiding her well enough both from the treacherous illuminations of the moon, and also from the eyes of the Prince. He seemed to be carefully watching the water for any movement. Sitheia could see his hand gripping the hilt of his sword. Every time she has seen the Prince before, he always looked so nice and kind. The tension that he was displaying now scared her.

Finally the Prince seemed to have decided that the sound that he heard must have been from an animal. He removed his hand from the hilt and soon after he left.

Sitheia was finally able to breathe out.

Her racing heart that was not accustomed to so much excitement as she had this night was beginning to slow down. She waited a while longer before she got out of the water. In a hurry she put on her armor and returned to the village without being seen by anyone.

She planned on having a little chat with John. He said that this place was a secret. If it was a secret, than why so many people were coming and going through it.

Later that night, when Sitheia was laying in her bad her mind went back to the events that happened at the pool. She brought her fingers to her lips when she remembered the kiss that she shared with Katherine. It was her first kiss.

Despite her lack of experience with kissing, she was sure that that was not an ordinary kiss. Something else happened in that pool.

An image of both Katherine and John appeared in front of her eyes and that put a smile on her face. She later fall asleep feeling happy and content. They were both hers.

CHAPTER 12

Darkness engulfed her from all sides. There was no up and down. There was no left and right. Everywhere, everything was the same. Darkness was everywhere.

Sitheia wanted to touch her face to make sure that her eyes were there and that they were open, but she couldn't move in any way with any part of her body. She could not blink not that it would have made a difference, because there was not even a spark of light around her to give her any sense of where she was or what was going on. She tried to scream, but no sound came out of her mouth. There was nothing. She was in an empty endless Void, lost and forgotten.

She existed like that in the Void in a place where there

is no time. There is no life or death. There are no senses and Sitheia understood. She couldn't see anything because there was nothing for her to see. In the emptiness that was everywhere there was nothing and no one. Only the spark of her soul still burned bright. She was alone, again. This is not what she wanted. She never wanted this.

Sitheia woke up screaming. She tried to lift herself up. Bumping her head she realized that she was not in her own bed. She made sure that her eyes were open, but just like in her dream there was nothing to see. The world around her was dark. But, there was something different now. She was aware that this was not the Void. She was certain that now there was a world around her.

She was on her back laying and she was grateful that she could feel the cold stone under her skin. It was ruff and it smelled... She couldn't smell anything. Wherever she was, there was no air in here. She could not breathe.

Panic got hold of her and she tried to push whatever was that it was above her. But, she couldn't. It seemed to be another stone wall, on all sides around her. How did she get here? Was she going to die? She wasn't certain. She could not feel the emptiness in her lungs. She could not even hear the sound of her heartbeat. Was she dead already? She tried to scream again. No sound came from her mouth, because there was no air left in her to form the words, but she could still feel the screams inside her head.

Then the world around her started to shift. The tomb disappeared and she was in some kind of hall with many columns and large windows. There were a lot of people, but she couldn't see them clearly. They were more like blurs of shadows, lights and colors. At the end of the hall in front of some kind of throne, a tall man in plated armor was standing looking at the assembled men. The armor was black with a yellow cape, but was shining so strong as if the Sun itself was reflected from it. Above and behind him, on the wall there was a shield with an image of two crossed swords underneath the Sun. Over the shield there were the largest antlers that Sitheia has ever seen.

From all the people in the crowded hall, only the man in front of the throne was clearly visible. His face was so strange, so angular that it looked like the bones on his face made angles sharp enough for a person to cut himself on them. The skin around his eyes was grey and his eyes were like two lamps of coal sunken deep into the skull and they were looking right where Sitheia was.

"Find me that witch!" Deep strong voice echoed through the hall and Sitheia could swear that his eyes were glowing red.

When Sitheia opened her eyes she was lying in her bed and there was a damp cloth on her forehead and on her chest under her nightgown. She let out a sigh. It was just a dream.

She tried to prop herself on her elbow, but a hand pushed her down. It was Mrs. Agnes.

"Calm down, Sitty. It's all right. It's all right." She spoke with a soothing voice.

"Mrs. Agnes? What is going on? What are you doing here?" Sitheia asked looking around.

She was in her own bed, but she was wearing a different nightgown than her usual one. The smell of vinegar pinched her nose. The cloth that was on her forehead and the one she had on her chest were both damp with vinegar. Mrs. Agnes was sitting on a chair next to her bed with a bowl filled with vinegar and she was preparing another cloth. Several candles were lit and Sitheia could see that there was no one else in the room except for Miss. Olivia, the Alchemist's cat.

"Hush, child. You had fever. You gave us a fright." She said. "You were burning with fever. Your mother and I have been trying to cool you down for three days."

"Three days?"

"Yes. Your temperature just started to come down."

"I don't remember anything. I went to bed and… nothing."

"You've been in a delirium because of the high temperature. How did you get sick? I remember that you were fine three days ago." Agnes asked with Miss. Olivia rubbing herself from her leg.

Sitheia tried to recall the events before she went to bed. She remembered the pool and the moment she had with Katherine.

"I was at the pool that is filled with the water that comes out of the Temple." Sitheia said.

"But Sitty, no one ever goes there. That place is off limits."

"I may not have heard that part." Sitheia started. "I was kind of stressed and I thought that a swim in the pool will relax me."

"Sitty! That water is heavily enchanted. When you go to the temple for purification, your body first goes through a ritual of preparation before you can go in the water."

"I know."

"To go into the water without preparation can get you to go mad." Mrs. Agnes who was a mentor to Sitheia as well her friend sounded a bit disappointed at her foolishness.

"I am sorry. I didn't know that all of this was going to happen as a result." Sitheia felt embarrassed because all of this that happened was a result of her not wanting to go through the regular path through the temple. "You have no idea what a terrible dream I just had."

"About what?"

"It wasn't like any other dream that I've had." Sitheia said and thought a bit about the dream she had about the vampire and the werewolf. "It felt like it was really happening."

Mrs. Agnes listened carefully as Sitheia told her all about her dream and when she finished with her story they sat quietly for a while until the cat draw their attention. Miss. Olivia not liking to be ignored scratched Agnes's leg to remind her that she was here. The herbalist cursed, grabbing the cat for the skin on the back of her neck and lifting her in front of her eyes.

"Auuu! Miss. Olivia, you bad cat! Get out of here! Go home!" She yelled and dropped the cat away from her.

Weather Miss. Olivia was insulted or not, she dashed up the stairs and disappeared.

"I should get your parents. Your family has been extremely worried. We all were." Agnes said and went toward the stairs that led to the upper floor. Before she started on the stairs, Agnes turned back toward Sitheia. "Hey, Sitty. You may not want to worry your parents with the details of your dream, they are pretty upset already."

Sitheia followed her with her eyes until she could no longer see her. She was right of course. Three days. How could this happen to her? Agnes said that she had a fever, but why? How? There is no way it could be because of the enchanted water, was there? She felt so good when she went to bed. It was all so strange.

Next, her thoughts were interrupted by a pair of hands that went around her. Her little sister was crying while she was hugging her.

"You scared me. Promise me that you are never going to do that to me again. You got it? Promise." Dana was talking at a rapid pace as she pulled herself from the hug to look at her big sister.

"I promise." Sitheia accepted looking into her sister's watery eyes, before her eyes fell on her ashen faced parents. "Mom? Dad?"

"Baby, you scared the hell out of us." Her mother said hugging her.

"We were so worried." Her father said as he put away the cloth that has fallen of her forehead so that he can give her a hug.

"I am really sorry." She said.

"It's not your fault honey. People get sick." Her father said.

"Agnes said that you've been swimming in the pool behind the temple." Her mother said, Sitheia wasn't sure if that was a question or an accusation.

"Wait. You know about the pool? I thought that nobody knew about that place." Sitheia said.

"Ahem… ahem…" Her father cleared his throat in a meaningful way. "You know that you did not invent the world? It existed for long time before you were born, dear." Her father said with a kind smile that made her feel silly.

"That place exists since the building of the temple."

Her mother added. "It is a place where all the water that is being enchanted in the temple is gathering before the river takes it to the sea. Everybody knows that."

"Then, how come I've never heard of it?" Sitheia said pulling herself in a sitting position in the bed. "I thought that it was a secret place."

"That's cute, Sitty." Her dad said. "You've never heard of it, because that is a place that should not be visited by anyone. So it is best if people don't even know about it. That place is so dangerous, as you were able to see for yourself. People who have been exposed to that water have gone mad. Some have even died from the experience. You were very lucky to have survived." Her father sounded stern, but his face could not hide the worry. Her parents have truly feared for her life while she was in that state somewhere between sleep and death.

Sitheia didn't know what else to say other than:

"I am sorry. I really am. I didn't know that this was going to happen. You got to believe me." Sitheia said with tears starting to run down her cheeks.

"We know, honey. We know." Her mom said hugging her.

"We are just glad that you're fine." Her dad agreed and joined the hug.

CHAPTER 13

In the days that followed Sitheia recovered fully. She even started helping her parents again in the family shop. She didn't like working in the shop any more than before she went swimming in the pool, but she had a guilty conscience for worrying her family. She also worked at the Inn, but it also didn't help her rising temper. Sitheia did her best to keep her head down, at least for a while. But the fact remained that she didn't have the temper for this kind of work. And spending more time in the shop only made her irritable again. Soon her practice of archery in the backyard wasn't enough to pull her thoughts away from the fact that she hasn't been to see the Door for so long.

It also didn't help that word around the village

has spread about her being sick after swimming in the forbidden pool. There were even some rumors that she has already gone mad.

One morning she decided that it was time to draw the line and she did it while she was having breakfast with her family. Because she felt that she was about to test the theory about the Cat people not being able to hurt another person and she would hit some drunken customer at the Inn.

"Tomorrow I am going hunting." She declared while chewing on her beans.

Her mother lifted her head from her food.

"I thought we talked about this. It is not fitting for a woman to be hunting. It is bad enough what you are doing behind the house." said Mary.

Sitheia expected that her mother would react like this and thought that she was prepared for a quarrel to defend her position, but something changed her mind. She saw an image of the Door in her mind and she knew.

"This is not a discussion. I have made up my mind. I am going tomorrow and that's it. I just thought that you should know." Her words were calm and cold leaving no room for any prolonged discussions or any other dialogs on the subject.

Her mother did not respond and just continued to eat in silence.

"All right, then. If you are insisting that you are to go

hunting, than you can't go alone. It is too soon after your incident at the pool. You may get sick while you are out there and there will be no one around to help you. You wouldn't even be able to send word that you need help."

"Mom, I am not going to get sick again."

"How do you know that? You don't." Her mother said. "I know that you are grown up now and you feel like you can make decisions by yourself, but if you are out there all by yourself, I will go mad from worry."

Sitheia wasn't sure how to respond to that. She felt great and she was almost certain that she was not going to get sick, but she understood her mother's worry. From one side she knew that hunting required sneaking around and moving quietly, but on the other side if she did go alone her parents will be worried sick.

"It is your first time going hunting. I can come with you and show you where to find game and how not to get noticed." George offered help.

"Thanks, dad. But, I need to do this by myself without your help. But, so you can be at ease you should know that I will not be going by myself. I will take John with me."

"Are you sure? To find some game, you may need to go further away from Sacred Pools. If you go too far, you may not be able to return before nightfall. And about your intention to take John with you, I know that he is strong and he is very devoted to you, but he has never been in the woods. He has no experience of how to behave in a forest. He might not be the right companion for you."

"I am sure. I'll bring my backpack with me. If night falls on me, I will make camp and return the next day. I am taking John because it will be good for him and for me, and it will make you feel better knowing that I am not alone."

"Very well. May the Goddess bless you with a bountiful hunt." Her father blessed her.

"Yes, a bountiful and delicious hunt." Her mother agreed.

Sitheia expected a lot more resistance from her parents. But, now that the part of her plan that was convincing her parents was done, next she needed to make sure that John was willing to go hunting with her.

* * *

When she came to see John, Sitheia first had to convince him that she wasn't mad at him. John kept apologizing for telling her about the pool and that he had no idea that the water was dangerous. Sitheia waved off his concern focusing more on the coming hunt.

"Are you sure that you want to go hunting so soon after spending three days in what did Agnes said it was called?" John said.

"A coma. And yes, I do want to go." Sitheia said.

Sitheia always got nervous when she had to explain why she had to go to the woods. The thing was that if she tell people that she needed to see the Door, they will all think that she was either crazy if they were feeling generous or they'll think that she was cursed or something. The Cat people were big on believing in curses.

"Why? Why do you feel that you have to go now?" He asked and looked at her. Her face said it all. She was debating in her head if she should tell him the true or not.

"Listen Sitty. You've been nice to me, nicer than anyone ever has. I feel the kind of love and loyalty toward you that is difficult to explain, the kind that I don't have for anyone else. If you ask me, I would follow you to the deepest parts of the Underworld. And I am not exaggerating. I mean every word. All I ask from you is not to treat me as one of the other Cat that may or may not judge your actions. By default, I will agree with you no matter what. I don't think that I ask a lot by wanting for you to be honest."

"I am sorry John for doubting you for even a second." Sitheia said and then she stopped.

"Well? What is it?"

After a short silence Sitheia spoke.

"I need it." She said. "I haven't been to visit the tower and see the Door for so long. It almost physically hurts the pull that I feel. I just want to drop everything and just go there as fast as possible."

"So going hunting is just an excuse for you to go to the tower?"

"In a way, but not exactly." Sitheia wanted to explain it clearly to John. "I do wish to go hunting. You know how much I am practicing archery in the backyard? The reason for it is because right before I release the arrow, I feel as the world stops for a moment. In that moment when I am fully focused on the target I feel so calm and so peaceful, it is hard to explain it. All the annoyance, all the stress and tension that I feel, in that single moment, all of it is gone."

"You hate working in the shop, don't you?" John said it directly. "Just admit it. I can tell that you are close to strangling some of the people that you are dealing with at work."

Sitheia just smiled and lowered her eyes. She felt embarrassed a bit for feeling that way, but also she felt glad that John understood her and she didn't have to pretend with him.

"I am struggling with the possibility of doing that for the rest of my life, John. As a matter of fact, I don't want to do anything specific for the rest of my life. What is the point of it all, if I am to live a life where days are repeating each other in an unending loop?"

"What is the alternative? Live everyday as if there is no tomorrow?"

"Of course, not. We are not animals. But, also we are not slaves as well. Life should have some general direction in which it will be going, but it should have some parts that are left to be discovered."

"I don't think that is correct." John said.

"What is not correct?" Sitheia looked at him not understanding his objection.

"Well, technically. We are slaves, in a way." John said, but Sitheia was making a face that indicate that she wasn't following him, so he moved on to elaborate. "The bargain, the deal that our ancestors have made with Lord Perdival."

"What about the bargain?"

"Well, the bargain obligates all of their descendants, meaning us, to serve all future Lords of Perdival in exchange for their protection."

"But, that is a mutually beneficial arrangement. It is not enslavement."

"Our people willing have entered into their servitude, but the fact remains that we do everything that they tell us. We build their buildings, produce their food, and empty their chamber pots. Have you ever seen a Cat refuse to obey an emissary, ever?"

Sitheia tried to remember an event where some of her countrymen have refused to obey a command from their overlords, but she couldn't remember a single event.

"I haven't. In fact, our people looked happy even excited to obey no matter what is asked from them."

"Exactly." John said. "Our masters are not violent. They don't kill us at whim. They don't beat us or torture us. But, just because they are not evil masters, that doesn't make them any less our masters."

Sitheia patted his large back.

"You've been thinking about this a lot, have you?"

"It's been bothering me for a while."

"How long?"

"Since I met you."

Sitheia gave him a doubtful look.

"I am serious. Since I met you, I've been having rebellious thoughts."

"Rebellious?" Sitheia smiled, she liked the sound of that word.

"Yes. I am not sure. But, if a Lord asks me to do something, and you tell me to do something opposite, I think that I will do what you have told me to do."

"Really?"

"Really."

Sitheia and John looked at each other for a long time without saying anything. They had a special connection. It was not like friends or lovers or family, it was much deeper than that. Sitheia couldn't find the word for it, but she knew that now she had something similar with Katherine, the acolyte. After a while spent in silence, she pulled his head toward her and put a kiss on his forehead.

"I know what you need. A hunt" She said smiling. "The trill of stalking an animal, killing it and eating it is a rear feeling. You are coming with me, tomorrow. You are up for it?"

John smiled feeling much better.

"As you command, my lady." He said with a mock bow, but she liked it anyway.

"Do you have some kind of weapon?" Sitheia asked.

"No. But, I'll ask the guards if I can borrow something."

"Good. Tomorrow before dawn, I'll wait for you on the meadow at the base of the tower."

"As my lady wishes." He bowed again.

The conversation left both of them in a good mood. Sitheia was so happy that tomorrow she was going to be hunting and she was going to be visiting her silent friend that she walked with a bounce.

Sitheia spent the rest of the day helping at home around the house. It was more for the purpose of calming her nerves, than for anything else. She was so excited that she could barely eat her dinner.

Before going to bed, while Sitheia prepared her backpack for the hunt her mother packed her some fresh bread, two apples and a waterskin.

"You may be searching for animals near the river. Be careful on the stones nearby. The water makes them slippery and all sorts of little creatures may hide in there such as snakes." Her mom said making Sitheia smile in appreciation that her mother has come to terms with her decision.

"Don't try to hunt something that is too big for you to carry back and always be on the move. A hunter is never like a rock. Before your arrow hits, you need to be in a different position ready to fire another. John will be with you. But even between the two of you, you won't be able to carry back too big an animal unless you plan on dragging the carcass for days. So, look for smaller animals." Her father was trying to give her as many advices as he could in the short time he had. "If you wound an animal, you must track it down and kill it. It is an unnecessary cruelty to let the animal suffer until it dies on its own. And don't forget, we hunt so we can eat. Don't kill more than we need. If you want to practice, do it on the target in the backyard, not on animals. When you are about to release an arrow, think of the food that beast will provide. Being motivated in that way, you'll have higher chance of hitting the target."

All that Sitheia was able to do was smile and nod at all the advices she got from both of her worried parents, hoping that she'll remember at least something.

"Leave her be, you two." Her grandpa called at them from near the fireplace. "She'll do fine and better than fine. When she is out there, her instincts will take over and probably she won't remember a word of what you're saying."

That made Sitheia smile nervously, probably because

she feared that it might be true.

"Thank you both. But, don't worry. I'll be fine." She gave both of them a hug.

CHAPTER 14

That night she was having an amazing dream. It looked so real, Sitheia felt that it must have been real. She was hunting and a bear came out in front of her, just like the bear that her grandpa killed. The bear spotted her and started running toward her, roaring with an open jaw. But, Sitheia wasn't afraid. On the contrary, she was calm and cold. She knocked an arrow and pulled the bowstring. When she released it, the arrow hit the bear right between the eyes and the bear fell before her feet.

Sitheia then grabbed the fur behind the neck of the bear with one hand and dragged the bloody corpse to the ruined tower and dropped it in front of the Door. Sitheia looked at the Door and spoke:

"This is for you".

At that, the Door started glowing brighter and brighter until Sitheia wasn't sure any more if there was any door behind the light.

Sitheia woke up all sweaty and bursting with energy. It was still very dark and the sun seemed to be far from rising, but Sitheia felt that it was time to go. She got dressed and made sure that she had everything she needed in her backpack before she threw it over her back. With the bow and the quiver with arrows in her hands she sneaked out of the house making sure that she did not woke up anyone.

She took a deep breath of the spring air that smelled like flowers. Even though the winter has passed, this early in the morning the air was still chilly. Sitheia adjusted her new armor. It fitted her perfectly. She was able to move with ease, but her body was still protected. Sitheia had to admit that this year's gifts were awesome.

She saw a guard with a torch on the other side of the street, but since she wasn't feeling very chatty, Sitheia decided to dive into the shadows. She crouched and moved stealthily into the darkness of the night. And before you can say "Sitheia is an awesome hunter", she was on the other side of the river getting out of Sacred Pools. She moved through the farmed plots of land to avoid the guard patrol and then she started climbing.

Going to the tower from the usual way would have

been so much easier, but it would have taken her at least an hour more. If she didn't had the armor she might have taken the longer path. But with this light armor on, she felt safer.

Her estimations about how many things she should pack were on target. The backpack contained everything she might need for a day or two hunting in the forest without weighing her too much so it didn't hinder her ability to climb or move silently and quickly.

The village was almost entirely in darkness with only several torches from the guards breaching the black sea. So all she had for illumination was the light from the stars and the moon. Fortunately, Sitheia has been climbing these rocks for most of her life and by now she knew by heart where her feet should go and where her hands. Without any difficulty she used her muscles to pull herself in front of the ruined tower.

Looking at the tower by the light of the stars she wondered, how it must have looked when it was new and whole. What purpose did it serve? Was it just a watchtower, to be looking at the surrounding area, or was there something more to it?

To say that she was curious about this place was the understatement of the year. She ran her hand over several bricks that were still holding upright and smiled. Sitheia couldn't explain the connection she felt with this place, but she always felt better after spending some time in here.

She walked slowly over the spiral staircase as if she was walking over a staircase from some sparkling palace. The stars on the night sky were her chandeliers and the howling winds were her orchestra. Sitheia dressed in her leather armor walked toward the Door as if she was at a ball and was walking toward her dancing partner. The stars were reflected in her eyes as they saw the carvings on the Door. She has looked at the Door for years, every inch of it branded in her memory as if part of her identity.

"I dreamt about you." She said, greeting her friend with a smile. "I was hunting and I killed a bear. I brought it to you as a gift."

When Sitheia said that last part she suddenly felt sad that it wasn't true. That it was only a dream. But, she cheered up again.

"Don't worry. I am going hunting. I doubt that it will be a bear, but I will bring you a gift. I promise."

Sitheia sent the Door a kiss and returned to the base of the tower. She recognized the silhouette of John. He was waiting for her just a little beyond the meadow.

"You know, I have the feeling that soon you will be able to safely come and sit with me on this meadow." She called out to John.

"I will do what my lady commands, even if it leads me to my death."

"Stop being so melodramatic." She waved his concerns away. "Are you ready for the hunt?"

"I am." He said stepping out of the shadows of the trees.

The light of the stars combined with her eyes that have already somewhat adjusted to the night vision could see that John has gotten fully armed. In fact he looked like he was a moving armory. He was caring a spear and a small shield and when Sitheia came closer she spotted a short sword on his hip and a tiny axe on the other hip.

"Are you preparing to join the infantry?" She remarked on his gear.

John looked down at his weapons and shrugged.

"I borrowed these from the guards. I didn't know what to take and I am not very good with bows. So, I figured that I should take a spear and a sword just in case."

"What's with the axe?"

"For firewood, of course." John said as if it was obvious.

"It's fine by me. Only, will you be able to keep up with all that steel on you?"

"Don't worry. I will."

For a moment she considered in what direction they should be moving. Going by the river was a good way to find beasts. But, somehow she doubted that they were going to find any animals this close to the village. She figured that they should be moving parallel to the river going away from Sacred Pools and that is what they did.

The sun woke up and went up in the sky and Sitheia still hasn't killed anything. She saw a dear twice, but the dear saw her too and run off. Crouching near she saw several ducks and she knocked an arrow and draw the bowstring, but just when she was about to release the arrow a bird flew nearby and she released the arrow without seeing where it flew off. She missed and the ducks escaped.

Hunting turned out it wasn't as easy as shooting a target. Sitheia also noticed that sneaking around humans was a lot easier than around animals. It was as if they were able to both hear her and smell her far earlier than any human has. But, she was determined to find something. She was not going to return without a gift.

Finally, she saw a hare grazing grass carelessly. Sitheia was about to jump out from happiness that she saw it, but instead she crouched as near the ground as she could. She moved quietly and slowly trying not to scare off the little critter. Sitheia noticed that the air was moving from the rabbit toward her, so she knew that it would not be able to smell her. She stilled the arrow and aimed. Something cracked behind her and the rabbit ran off.

Soon it became apparent that as long as they are moving together, Sitheia won't be able to kill a thing. She had an opportunity to shoot a pheasant, but the bulky and noisy movements of John alerted the pheasant who took flight before Sitheia was able to even begin to aim. When later she spotted tracks of a rabbit in the soft ground and was eager to go and follow them, she had to slow down because John wasn't able to keep up under the weight of all those weapons. Finally she put a stop to the unnecessary waste of time.

"To be able to hunt, I need to move fast. No offense, John, but you are slowing me down."

"None taken. It's impossible to move any faster with all these weapons."

"That's OK. You will continue to move along the river and I will enter the woods and hunt something. When I am done, I will simply return to the river and I will track you down. Does that seem OK to you?"

"Yes. Yell if you need help."

"Sure. I will."

The moment Sitheia entered the woods by herself and she was no longer distracted by John's presence, her senses exploded. She was suddenly able to hear the entire forest around her. The rustling of leaves, the chirping and singing of numerous birds overlapped in a symphony of nature and life. For several moments that seemed to last for hours, Sitheia was so drunk on too much nature that she forgot about the hunt for a while.

Then, her eyes got fixed on the ground, on the little paw print which she followed to the next one and the next one. With her eyes on the ground and her bow in her hands, she moved fast over fallen tree branches and boulders. She felt as the tracks were getting fresher more and more. And she started to feel the excitement of getting closer to her target as an increase in her own pulse. Sitheia circled around a larger rock and was stopped in her tracks by a sound that she did not expect.

She heard a deep sound of heavy breathing from a bear that just happened to be resting nearby. Like blowing out a candle, in an instant her excitement was replaced by fear. The bear was lying some thirty feet from where Sitheia was standing and she was huge.

Sitheia wanted to believe that the bear still hasn't spotted that Sitheia was nearby, but she was wrong. With an irritated growl, the bear was already getting up. Sitheia could see that the bear was wounded. There were several patches of dark red blood on her fur. Very fast the heavy breathing turned into an upset growl as the bear rise up and turned toward Sitheia.

In an instant Sitheia had an arrow knocked and drawn aiming at the bear's head. She thought about her dream of killing a bear with a single shot to the head and chased the thought out of her head. There was no way that she can kill the bear with a single shot. And as strong and fast as the bear was, Sitheia would be dead before she can fire a second arrow. Running was also not an option. The bear would catch her and eat her. She had no clue of what to do.

With her heart pumping like mad, Sitheia backed down few steps. The bear followed growling louder. Nearby there was a large rock that she could climb on, but she would never get there in time. The bear stepped closer. For every three steps that Sitheia backed away, the bear would make one step to get closer. The distance between them was getting smaller. Those fangs did look enormous and dangerous, like tiny swords ready to chop her to pieces.

Sitheia had a terrible feeling that as her fear and panic grew. The anger in the bear's eyes grew with them. The bear stopped moving and roared loud enough to make Sitheia go deaf.

'Oh Goddess, she is going to attack. She is going to attack.' Thoughts of panic drove her crazy.

The bear let out another mighty roar and Sitheia saw the bear's body tense. She was about to attack her and Sitheia was going to die. So be it, at least she will try to take the bear with her. She pulled the drawstring as much as she could and was about to release it, when something hit the bear from the side. The bear roared in pain.

It was John. He hit into the bear while running at full speed with the shield up. The bear got dizzy from the hit, which gave them the time to start running toward the rock. John helped her climb and followed her up. By the time the bear recovered they were both hidden on top of the large rock. Lying flat to the surface of the rock and keeping as quiet as possible they waited for the bear to walk away. She roared several times, but gave up in the end and started moving away.

For a long time after they stopped hearing the bear, they waited quietly without moving.

"Do you think that she is gone?" Sitheia whispered.

"I have no idea." John shrugged his shoulders.

She looked at him. He has dropped his shield after he hit the bear, but his spear was missing too.

"Where is your spear?" She asked.

"I dropped it. When I heard the bear, I needed to come to you as fast as possible. The spear was slowing me down. I left it near the river."

Sitheia got up and tried to see as far as possible and could not see any sign of the bear.

"She must have left." Sitheia said.

"What on earth a bear is doing so close to the village?" John asked.

"I don't know. From what my grandfather and my father have told me, there shouldn't be any bears in this region. The closest they can be found is in the mountains at the edge of this land. There are caves in there."

"Why do you think that she has come down from the mountain? And do you think that there may be more?"

"I don't know. But, what I know for sure is that the

bear was wounded. I saw many bloody patches on her fur. The blood was dark and dry. Something must have chased her away from there."

"Like what?"

"Wyvern maybe. I don't know." Sitheia got of the rock first.

With John walking right behind her, Sitheia went to retrieve her bow. She didn't fire the arrow, so she retrieved it as well. John got his shield back. There was some blood on it.

Sitheia readied her bow and John draw out his sword. Looking out for the bear, they carefully got back to the river where John got his spear back.

"Next time we do this, I'll be taking fewer weapons." He said, but Sitheia waived at him to be quiet.

Before he was even able to turn and see what she was looking at, she pulled an arrow from her quiver and aimed. The image of the Door came in front of her eyes and her nerves calmed. She let out her breath as she released the arrow.

A heartbeat later, Sitheia pulled the arrow from the fur of the rabbit's neck with a smug smile. John congratulated her on her first kill. After several moments of exhilaration, she looked around and noticed that she didn't recognize the forest. It was obvious that if they followed the river, they will eventually get back to the village, but not one of the landmarks around them were familiar to them. They have gone further from Sacred Pools than they intended. The sun already started to go down for the day, so she knew that they will have to make a camp for the night.

"It will be dark in a few hours. We should find a secure place to set up camp for the night." She said.

"Do you think it's safe for us to sleep in here?" John asked.

"I don't know. The bear shouldn't have been here to begin with. She may return, or she may have moved on. But anyway, I wouldn't put our lives at risk if I can help it." Sitheia said. "That rock where we climbed to escape the bear. I think we should make camp next to it. We'll gather firewood and make fire. We can cook this rabbit for dinner. And if another bear shows up, we will be close enough to the rock to escape it. What do you think?"

"I know nothing about camping. So, I agree with everything that you are saying by default. Just tell me what to do and I'll do it." John said, fully confident that she had everything under control.

"All right, then. First, we'll return to the rock. I'll skin the rabbit and you can gather some firewood."

Sitheia felt guilty that her parents will be worried that she hasn't returned home the same day. They used what little light remained to gather firewood that they hopped was going to be enough to last them for the whole night.

They set up some makeshift barricades from fallen branches and rocks to impediment any intruder. Sitheia kept her bow nearby and John propped his spear and shield to one of the barricades keeping his sword at hand. From security standpoint, they were as safe as either of them knew how to prepare the camp.

John made a small circle of stones and started a fire in the middle. Following the recipe she learned from her father for cooking an animal in the forest she took out her sharp little knife and skinned the rabbit. She thought that her mother might actually be proud of how much she preserved the skin.

Next, she cleaned the rabbit of all the guts and skewered it with a sharp piece of wood. The cooking went almost smoothly with the rabbit falling over the fire only once. But, after she realized that she needs to have the rabbit high enough so it won't catch on fire, things went well. John making fun of her cooking skills didn't help her cook better, but at least it lightened the mood.

The meat was a little harder and stringier than when her mother was cooking a rabbit. But they were both hungry and tired and the meat was warm, so they had no complains. For her first kill it wasn't that bad and she said that.

"You know, for my first rabbit. This isn't that bad." She said looking at John and expecting for him to agree.

"Right." He said while putting some effort into biting off a piece of meat. "I have definitely had worse." He added.

"You have? Where?" She asked hopeful.

"I am sorry, I haven't. I just wanted to make you feel better." He said and she felt a little sad. "But, look on the bright side. This was your first kill and the first time you ever cooked. So, all in all, it's great." He said swallowing down a piece that was too hard to chew.

They battled with their meat for a while longer and afterward they drank some water from their waterskin. They made sure that the fire had enough firewood to last for a while, before they covered themselves with their cloaks and went to sleep with full bellies and a lot of happy thoughts.

CHAPTER 15

That night Sitheia had the craziest, strangest dream of her life and she was already becoming an expert of crazy dreams. It was dark and she was in a very tick forest. She could see herself with her back turned, kneeling and making weird sounds. When she turned and saw her own face, it was all bloody and filthy. She has been eating a raw rabbit, tearing at the flesh with her teeth and swallowing the pieces.

The whole dream felt so real, that Sitheia could feel the smell and could taste the blood. Eating that raw flesh in the dream made her feel better and more sated than eating the real rabbit that she cooked. She licked the blood that was dripping from her fingers. Then there was a strong light and the Door appeared in her dream and the whole Door was illuminated until it burst open.

Sitheia woke up startled and feeling like she is about to throw up, but she managed to suppress the feeling of nausea. She took a sip from her waterskin and felt a lot better.

The sky that was visible through the tree branches was still dark and her fire has gone out too. She shivered. Looking toward John, he was still sleeping and it was obvious that he was cold too. Sitheia realized that they have both come a little underprepared on their first hunting trip.

Sitheia considered building a new fire, but that would take so much more time and she didn't feel like wasting her time like that. She guessed that the dawn was near and that they will soon be getting ready for the journey back home. She started rubbing and stretching her arms and legs to loosen up her stiff muscles. As her muscles woke up, warmth started to build up inside them.

"Is the ground too hard for you, princess?" Sitheia scolded herself.

The scolding seemed to work because the aching in her muscles eased and her limbs stopped being so stubborn and answered her call to action.

"Who are you talking to, princess?" John said, making her turn to look at him.

He was awake and he was also massaging his own stiff

muscles.

"Shut up." She smiled throwing a small piece of firewood at him making him laugh out loud.

"It suits you, you know." He said getting a little more serious.

"What, a princess? No way. If I am to be a royalty, then I'll be a queen."

"Queen Sitheia? Hmm…" John tested how the title sounds.

"It doesn't sound right, does it? Empress Sitheia? Now, that sounds a lot better, don't you think?"

"Empress? Isn't that a bit much?" John wondered while getting up and dusting his cloak.

"Why? If I am dreaming, than at least I can dream big." Sitheia said checking the leftovers from the rabbit. "The dawn is close. We should eat and start getting back."

"The rabbit you caught yesterday is gone. You want to go back empty handed?"

"We won't go back empty handed. We'll catch something on our way back. In fact we need to catch at least two things."

"Why?"

"I promised the Door that I'll bring a gift."

John got tensed when he heard about the Door, but he had faith in Sitheia, so he said nothing.

"Is there anything left?" He said pointing at what used

to be her rabbit.

The rambling in her stomach made her remember the dream. Seeing herself eat the raw flesh, made her feel both sick and hungry. She poked at it and even took a bite, which she spit it out right away.

"It's disgusting. It wasn't this bad last night." She said.

"It was warm then."

"Now it's cold, hard and awful. When we get back, I will have to learn how to cook what I kill. Pity, it would have been a nice rabbit stew." She pulled her backpack and split the food that her mother has prepared for her in two. She handed half to John with a warning. "Not a word about this to my mother."

"I swear before the Goddess that I won't say a word." He swore with a smile as he took his food.

As much as she hated to admit it, Sitheia had to agree that this food was by far superior to her poor rabbit. It was a bit embarrassing for a hunter, to ruin her first kill with poor cooking. But there was nothing that she can do about it now. With a heavy breath Sitheia looked at the little fur of the rabbit. It was evidence that she has successfully hunted a rabbit. Then she remembered that her people didn't hunt for proofs of the kill, but for food.

With the first light of day, John made sure that the fire was entirely extinguished while Sitheia gathered their scattered belongings. John had his shield strapped to his back and the spear in his hands. She tossed the bag over her shoulders, grabbed her bow and started to look for something familiar that will tell her where exactly was she. Since she knew where the river was she set out in that direction, fully intending to refill her waterskin while she was there. She heard the river before she saw it. Her instincts told her to move quietly, so she signaled John to be quiet and they both crouched as they approached the end of the forest.

The fresh breeze hit her face as she approached keeping herself as low as possible, nearly blending in with a huge rock that was protruding from the ground where the forest ended. Together with the scent of fresh water Sitheia felt another smell. Stronger and a little musky.

She saw the two deer at the standing near the river bank. The one that was closer, grazed on the grass near the river, while the other was drinking from the water. Neither deer had noticed her.

Following her instincts, her arrow was knocked and ready to fly in the blink of an eye. But, she hesitated. She couldn't release the arrow. The teachings of her people would not let her kill the deer. The deer meant meat and a lot of meat at that. With one deer her family would have plenty of food, but she was too far from home.

Sitheia was not very strong and the deer was heavy. John was strong, but he was already burdened by his too many weapons. They wouldn't be able to carry it back home and there was no one nearby to help them carry it. They would either have to leave half of the meat behind which was a huge waste of meat or go looking for something else.

Not being able to kill the deer and at the same time not being able to let the opportunity slip, Sitheia was stuck in the moment. Her dilemma came to an end when she spotted a better target only several steps away from the deer.

The startled deer disappeared with several big leaps leaving Sitheia to pick up the rabbit with her arrow stuck in its neck. Smiling with pride, Sitheia bagged the rabbit.

"I could have bet that you were going to kill the dear." John said surprised.

"I was going to. But, then I remembered that we wouldn't be able to carry it back home. It's too heavy and we don't even have where to put the meat."

"We are a bit unprepared for this?" John suggested.

"You don't say." Sitheia sighed.

She lowered herself to the bank of the river and kneeled over the cool water. They both freshened up and refilled their waterskins while looking around for clues of their whereabouts.

The huge White Mountain which got her name because it was always white, meaning covered in snow, was difficult to miss. It was much closer now than when Sitheia was looking at it from her tower and it was on the other side of the river. That made things so much clearer about the direction that they should be moving toward.

The journey back was much more eventful than the first day of the hunt. Also it was much safer. They did not encounter any bears. But Sitheia managed to shoot down two pheasants. She moved fast. Crouched like a real cat stalking a prey with her bow always at the ready. John on the other hand, struggled to keep up with her. She ran through the forest much faster than him, but he always knew where she was. Running with the spear was not an easy thing to do. Following her was especially difficult because Sitheia was picking a path through the forest that was made out of protruding roots, fallen branches and large rocks.

Sitheia move very fast despite being so close to the ground and moving through a forest. She moved around bushes and over tree roots, fallen tree trunks and broken dry branches. Her habit of sneaking around and moving in secret through most of her life helped her to not make a sound as she slithered and glided over the terrain. Despite moving at such a speed, her eyes didn't stop darting in all directions looking for a movement. But, she didn't see anything until she got at the base of the ruined tower.

There it was. There was a squirrel, carelessly sniffing near the first steps of the spiral staircase.

"That is my tower." Sitheia whispered to herself with a tone of annoyance.

Her arrow found her mark as it was being guided by a magical force. Sitheia retrieved the arrow taking the squirrel with her as John arrived at the edge of the meadow panting.

"Were you running or flying through the forest? I could barely keep up with you." He said bending over to catch his breath. The spear fell off from his hand.

"Don't beat yourself up. You never stood a chance at keeping up with me." She teased with a smug smile. "Are you all right?"

"I am pitchy." He breathed out. "I just need a moment to catch my breath. You go. You do your thing with that magic tower and I'll wait for you in here."

"Come on, after everything we've been through. You have to come in. I am sure that she will let you get close." Sitheia protested.

John went pale.

"Please, Sitty. Don't make me go there. You saw how bad it was the last time."

Sitheia was not sure what to do. John was hers. The Door should have trusted him because of that. She closed her eyes and let her breath out trying to calm down, feeling the air and the breeze. Sitheia always believed that the wind was a way for the Door to communicate with her. When she opened her eyes she felt like she knew the answer.

"John." She said with a commanding voice clear as a

bell. "I won't ask you to come if you don't want to. But, I want to ask you something. Do you trust me?"

"Of course, Sitty. More than I trust anyone else in the world. You know that." John said firmly.

"Do you believe in me?" Sitheia said fixing him with her eyes.

The question sounded simple, but it didn't feel like that for John. He looked into her eyes and his features softened, his face relaxed.

"I do." He said and there was no doubt that he believed every word.

"Good. Then, take few steps forward and do what feels right to you, what seems natural for you. Just try it, please." Sitheia said.

Hesitantly John stepped forward. Nothing happened so he made another step and he kept walking forward toward Sitheia. It was as an invisible force was guiding him. His movements were instinctive without conscience intent.

When he stopped in front of her, he pulled out his sword and went down on one knee holding the sword as an offering to Sitheia.

"I John Cat of Sacred Pools hereby declare my allegiance to you Sitheia. I will follow you, serve you and protect you as long as I live." He spoke with a voice that seemed so unlike his own. When he finished he got up and hesitantly smiled at her.

"What was that?" Sitheia asked with wide opened eyes.

"I don't know." He shrugged with a shy smile. "I felt like that was the right thing to do. When we first met, I accepted that I was yours. Now, I believe that it is a bit more official."

"How do you feel? Are you OK or are you feeling dread again like the last time?" She asked looking for any sign that something may be wrong with him.

"No, actually I feel great. I think your tower has finally started to trust me."

She looked over her shoulders toward the beginning of the spiral stairs.

"Do you want to come up and see the Door?" She invited him.

"No. I don't want to push my luck. The day is half gone. I think I'll go back home and get some rest."

"Thanks for accompanying me on my first hunting trip."

"Well, I just swore my loyalty to you, so don't worry about it. It was my pleasure."

She untied the two pheasants that were strapped to her belt.

"Here, take these."

"Why?"

"They are your share of the hunt." Sitheia handed him the birds.

"You were the one who caught them."

"You saved my life with that bear. You more than earned them."

He took the pheasants, picked up the spear and was ready to go.

"I'll have to go and return the gear to the guards. I'll see you tomorrow."

"See you."

Sitheia waited a bit for him to disappear from her sight before she started to climb the stairs. She was sweaty and tired and she missed her soft and pretty bed that was stuffed with straw and covered with furs. In her mind she was already comfortably stretched over the bed and deep asleep.

As she climbed the spiral staircase she quietly sang a song for herself. She intended to bring the rabbit home, and to leave the squirrel as a gift to the Door. She was proud of herself. Simultaneously she managed to catch a gift for the Door and to keep her place free of intruders.

She smiled at the thought. Yes, this was her place. She had it claimed years ago and no one disputed her claim. Sitheia was the only person that ever came here and no one had such a connection to this beautiful old stones as she did. What John just did was a bit strange, with swearing allegiance to her and all. But at least the tower now trusted him. That was a good start.

"Yes, this is my place." She said testing how the words sounded when spoken out loud.

They felt good. They energized her body as she made the last turn and saw the most beautiful thing in the world.

CHAPTER 16

"I promised a gift and here it is." Sitheia spoke to the Door.

As always, she was the only one from the two of them doing the speaking. The Door never responded, but Sitheia always felt as if they were both communicating, just not in the way normal people do. She has never heard words, but she could tell if the Door agreed or disagreed with her. It was as if the wind was the Door's way to communicate with her.

Sitheia closed her eyes and spread her arms feeling the wind blowing at her back. It was stronger than ever before. It wasn't cold, but it was strong as if it was pushing her toward the edge of the tower.

Sitheia never doubted her friend so she stepped closer to the edge and looked up at the contours the wind was making. The sun was high in the sky and was making her squint. She couldn't take the piercing of the sunrays and she lowered her gaze toward Sacred Pools. The village was busy as always, with people rushing in different directions doing their many chores. It was a comforting and familiar view.

But then, out of the corner of her eye, she spotted something strange. The wind seemed to be blowing especially strong through the wheat field at the edge of the forest. It seemed like the whole field was moving. And then the wind suddenly stopped entirely. The wind stopped but the movement of the wheat field kept going on although a bit slower. That was very strange, for the field to be moving without wind. Sitheia thought that someone must have lost control over a herd of sheep.

She rubbed her eyes from the sting of the sun and looked better just to be sure at what she was looking at. The cool air at the top of the tower during the coldest winters that she could remember have never chilled her as much as what she saw.

Hidden among the crops there were armed men moving slowly toward her village. She couldn't see them well and for sure she didn't see them all, but she counted the disruptions in the usually perfect field. Sitheia counted at least four dozen and they all looked to be armed and scary.

'Bandits!' she thought. The village was about to be under attack and if the stories that her grandpa had told her were true, then the people were unable to defend themselves. There were several guards that patrolled the village but she didn't know if they could fight or not. But, what she did know was that even if they could fight, the guards were outnumbered three to one.

She had to warn the villagers just as the Door warned her.

"Thank you." She whispered turning toward her friend.

Sitheia removed the rabbit and the squirrel from her backpack and left them on the ground. She checked that her bow, her quiver and her backpack were secured before she started climbing down. This was not the safest way from the tower to her village, but it was the fastest. She got several scratches on her face, but the armor that she got for her birthday protected her body efficiently. As soon as her feet touched the ground she sprang into a run.

Since she was approaching Sacred Pools from a different direction than the bandits, there was no danger that they were going to notice that they've been discovered. Sitheia believed that they hadn't attack yet because they wanted to get as close as possible without being detected and to catch the villagers off guard. She considered yelling to warn the villagers, but she feared that the panic her warning might cause will force the bandits to attack sooner which will result with more casualties.

Running faster than she ever has in her entire life, Sitheia had to jump over a child that was playing near the bridge and almost run into an old man. She had no time to turn and apologize so she didn't and just kept running.

She was without a breath when she got to the home of the Village Elder. The Village Elder was several years older than her grandfather. He was of middle height and very skinny. Despite losing a lot of his muscle mass from aging, he still had enough strength to be able to do his duties as a leader.

When Sitheia got to his house, he was sitting on a bench in front of his house with several other people whom Sitheia recognized as the people who were in charge of agriculture for the Cat. All of them were at least thirty years younger than the Village Elder and they seemed to be worried about a possible cold wave. They all got startled when they saw Sitheia running at breakneck speed toward them. They all shook their heads as if waking from a dream, before lowering their brows at the rude disruption.

"Aren't you the daughter of George, the hunter?" One of the men asked her.

"She is. I know George. He wouldn't raise a daughter

that interrupts her elders when they are talking about serious matters." Said another.

"Why are you running like that? You may hurt someone." A third man added.

Sitheia had no time for arguing or listening to lessons about manners and good behavior. She had a very good reason for running. Sacred Pools didn't have a lot of time before the bandits attack. She didn't have the luxury of being nice and polite.

"SHUT UP!" She yelled at the elders startling everyone including herself.

While the other men were still confused by her strange behavior, the Village Elder recognized that Sitheia wouldn't behave like this if she didn't have a good reason for it.

"What is it, girl? What has happened?" He asked with a raucous voice weakened by age, but strengthened by the weight of his duties and responsibilities.

Sitheia was grateful that he wanted to listen to her problem, because her problem was everyone's problem. Sitheia forced herself to calm down and to start pushing the words out.

"Bandits! I saw them hidden in Florian's crops. Armed and heading this way."

"In my crops?" One of the men jumped from the bench. "I checked the fields before lunch, there was no one there."

"Are you sure of what you have seen?"

One after the other the men got off the bench with fear evident on their pale faces.

"I am sure." Sitheia was getting angry at the pointless waste of valuable time.

"How many?" The Village Elder cut off the others from making any more comments.

"I counted about four dozen. Maybe there were more that I didn't see. I didn't raise the alarm out of fear that they may attack sooner." Sitheia talked fast.

"Four dozens?"

"Goddess saves us."

"What do we do?" They all turned toward the Village Elder looking for a solution.

"We have to inform the castle." The Elder said with determination. "They will send an army to destroy the attackers."

"But, if the bandits are this close, they'll never get here in time."

"We are going to organize the people and do our best to stall the bandits as long as possible. We can't fight off the bandits, but we can slow them down. We will barricade every entrance to the village. Dealing with the barricades will delay the attack. You must ride to the coast and send a message to the castle." The Village Elder spoke to Sitheia.

"Me? I... I don't know how to ride."

"You'll figure it out. You managed to get here in time to warn us, you will find a way to call for our master's protection." The Village Elder said and raised his hand to stop the objections from both Sitheia and from the men around him who all started to open their mouths to protest. "We will buy you as much as time as possible."

Sitheia was too stunned to say anything, she just nodded in agreement.

"Matt! You will take Sitheia to the stable and you'll give her a horse while I wrote a message." The Village Elder said to the man on his right.

"Right away, sir."

Matt guided Sitheia around the Village Elder's house where the stable was. He pushed the door open and took the bewildered girl to where a tall chestnut was resting. Sitheia who has never approached a horse felt a little scared by the giant creature which was so much bigger than her and could very easily step on her.

But, lives were at stake. The lives of everyone she ever knew, including her family. She listened to Matt's instructions and next she was riding on top of the horse. Matt led the horse to the front of the Village Elder's house where the Elder was waiting with a small scroll in his hand.

"I don't think I need to point out that all of our lives depend on you getting that message in time." The Village Elder said as he gave her the scroll.

Sitheia nodded and she nudged the horse forward. As every time before, Sitheia surrendered to her instincts. She pushed the horse forward and the horse responded by galloping as fast as he could. Sitheia held herself close to the horse and hoped that she'll get there in time. She also hoped that she won't be thrown off the horse.

She has never been to the beach, but she knew the general direction and the road didn't have any intersections so there was nothing to confuse her. By the sharp salty air she recognized that the sea was getting closer.

Sitheia made one more turn and she came out on the sandy beach. She could see the castle standing in the water far from where she was standing. But, on the beach right in front of her, there was a large building that was elevated from the sand by wooden columns. She climbed off the horse and stepped toward the building.

She has never even seen sand, let alone walk over it. It felt weird to Sitheia that her feet were going so deep in the sand. It was difficult to walk on the beach but she had to push on and bring help to the village. Sitheia climb the steps and was just about to reach for the door, when the door opened inwardly.

CHAPTER 17

Sitheia found herself staring at the palest shade of blue eyes that she has ever seen, crowned by two black eyebrows and a large forehead. His black hair was long enough that it went down until it reached his jaw. The man had the palest skin that she has ever seen, so pale that it was almost translucent. Sitheia swallowed her saliva. It was an emissary. Dressed in a long black coat with several columns of large red buttons, he looked intimidating.

"Sitheia? What are you doing here?" He said.

The emissary fixed her with his pale eyes. When he lowered his brows he looked even more intimidating than before, but Sitheia had no time to be fearful. Sacred Pools had no time. The funny thing was that he knew her by the name and he recognized her even though she has never even seen him in her entire life.

"You know my name, my lord?" Sitheia asked hesitantly.

"Of course I know your name, Sitheia. My name is Lord Faust. I was the one who brought you to this world." He said making Sitheia drop her jaw.

"What?"

"Don't you know that you are the First child?"

"I do, but what that has to do with you my lord?"

"A lot, but I don't believe that you are here for a history lesson. Why have you come, Sitheia?" He asked her again. The way he spoke, it felt like every word of his was a command. But, his question reminded her about the immediate threat that her people were facing.

"My lord, bandits are going to attack Sacred Pools. They may already have. The Village Elder sent me to deliver this message so that the castle can send help." She said turning over the letter from the Village Elder.

Lord Faust took the letter and read it quickly. When he finished reading it he looked toward the sky.

"Cursed sun. You should come inside." He said. "I have to send a message to the castle."

He stepped aside leaving her enough room to get in what seemed to be a long hallway with several doors left and right. There were several small chandeliers that were made of iron. The planks that made the walls were not painted. The light from the candles was dim and they illuminated a depressingly empty hallway with no decorations on the walls. There were no coat hangers next to the door. The place felt like no one lived there.

Sitheia has never before entered a building that belonged to the Lords of Perdival. She wasn't sure what she expected from the inside of the building, but this empty hallway was definitely not what she imagined.

"You are not impressed?" Lord Faust smirked and started to lead her down the hallway.

"No." Sitheia said a little confused. "It's just that this is not what I expected."

"And what did you expected to see?" Lord Faust seemed amused.

"I am not sure." She was honest. "Everyone that I have ever seen from the castle is so nicely dressed, that I thought…"

She went quiet, feeling that she has said more than a Cat should say.

"Well, you still haven't seen any of our buildings." He said getting to the end of the hallway and turning left. "This is our embassy. More like an outpost. Hardly anyone is ever here, so there is no point in decorating the place."

"My lord, what about the help for Sacred Pools?" Sitheia dared to remind the Lord about the dire condition in which her village was in.

"Here we are." He said and opened the first door to the right.

The room where they entered was like no other room that she has ever been to. It was double times the size of their entire home for one thing. There were no beds in it or a kitchen table. There was a fireplace, but it was not burning. In one corner of the room there was a bookcase filled with books and there was an armchair next to it. But, this was not a wooden armchair like the one that her grandfather liked to sit on, but it was soft and looked like it was a bed made for sitting.

The other side of the room was mostly occupied by a giant dark brown desk that was much bigger than any desks that she has ever seen. Behind the desk there was something resembling a throne.

"Is that a throne?" Sitheia asked awed by the strange room. Her question made Lord Faust laugh melodically.

"A throne? No, that is my chair and this is my office. You can sit over there." Lord Faust said pointing at two smaller chairs in front of the desk. "You can help yourself with some candies."

On the desk there were many things, mostly papers, but there was also a plate of candies in different colors. Most of them were dark red, but there were also green and white and pink. Sitheia reached out to help herself.

"Not the red ones. They are for me only." Lord Faust said with his back turned. He was bent over some device that looked like a ball made of glass. Sitheia returned the red candy and took a white one. It had an amazing taste. "You like that one? It's vanilla."

"It's good."

"Do you want to see some magic?" He said holding a small piece of paper in his hand. Sitheia nodded.

Lord Faust turned toward her brushing his hair from his eyes. He held the piece of paper on the palm of his hand in front of him. His entire eyeballs turned red. The palm holding the paper started to glow bright and just before Sitheia started to feel the need to cover her eyes, the glow turned into a blue flame that went up from his palm. The flame burst tall and strong consuming the paper. When the flame went out there was no trace from the paper left. Lord Faust's eyes turned back to the pale blue color and on his hand there was no sign that there ever was a fire.

Sitheia reminded herself to close her mouth. That was the first time she saw a spell being cast in front of her. It was flashier and more colorful than she expected. Also the way his eyes changed color while he was casting the spell. Does it always happen that way? She had millions of questions that she wanted to ask, but the pressing threat to her village took precedence.

Lord Faust took his sit behind the desk and popped

one of the red candies in his mouth. He must have really liked those candies because the look of relief that he got on his face was not the kind that Sitheia associated with eating a candy. That kind of relief that was borderline pleasurable she could only associate with something like ten hours of sleep, or maybe a drink of cold water after a hot summer's day.

"Lord Faust? I am sorry for being persistent, but when are you going to send the message?" Sitheia asked.

"I already did." He said with a smirk. "We are waiting now for their answer."

Sitheia did not wish to push her luck, but she didn't know if she was ever going to get the chance to get some answers, so she tried.

"Lord Faust? Would you mind telling me about what you meant when you said that you were the one who brought me to this world, sir?"

The emissary took another candy and put it in his mouth, before looking up at Sitheia.

"I guess that may not be entirely correct. Mary Cat, your mother was the one who carried you. And there was a midwife that also played a role in the delivering of the baby Sitheia. I had a different role in your creation."

"What kind of role?" Sitheia had trouble understanding anything that the Lord was saying.

"Well, I made sure that your parents got together for

one thing. When your mother got pregnant, I followed your development with little tweaks to make sure you stay alive." He said with a serious expression. Lord Faust seemed a little distant as if in his mind he was going through the events that led to her birth. "You must already know that before you were born there were seven years of drought?"

Sitheia nodded not wanting to interrupt the story.

"In that period not one baby was born. There were so few conceptions and before your mother not one pregnancy lasted more than a month. It was a trying time. We had to think a little out of the box. We did what we could and our efforts bore fruit. And that fruit turned out to be you."

Sitheia have heard thousand times the story about the birth of the First baby. But she has never heard this part of the story. It made her wonder what they have done, to make sure that she is born.

"With you coming to this world, I had to make a few things that insured that there are more babies coming after you. And they did. The Cat population has been growing at a very desirable rate." Lord Faust seemed so proud of himself with whatever he did to insure that the Cat have more babies.

As Sitheia was thinking about the unusual and very mysterious circumstances that made her birth possible and Lord Faust was having another red candy, a blue flame burst right in front of the emissary. The flame looked just like the one that Lord Faust conjured. Only this one was not on top of his palm but in midair.

Lord Faust looked like he was expecting it. He plunged one hand into the flame and when he pulled it out he was holding a piece of paper in it. The flame disappeared just as suddenly as it appeared. Lord Faust scanned the paper and nodded with satisfaction as he crumbled the paper in his fist.

"That was a message from the castle. They are mobilizing. They expect the regiment will be in Sacred Pools in a few hours."

"Few hours?" Sitheia went pale. "But, my people may as well be dead by then."

Lord Faust made an apologetic face.

"That is the fastest that they can get across from the island. They understand the gravity of the situation, but there is nothing that can be done to speed it up. I am sorry." He sounded honest which infuriated Sitheia.

She got of the chair with her hands in her hair trying to focus. Her family, her parents, her sister, her grandpa, John, Katherine, Mrs. Agnes, Mr. Olaf, everyone. They appeared in front of her eyes one by one and she felt that if she doesn't go to be with them, that she might never see them again.

"I have to go. I have to be with my family." She whispered.

"That is not very wise." Lord Faust said.

"I don't care if it is wise or not. I have to go. I have to help them." She said pacing over the room.

"How will you help them? You are a Cat, are you not? You can't fight. You will just be one more potential casualty." He sounded as if he was talking about her going to help with the harvest or not, or maybe for apple picking. Didn't he understand that the lives of her family were at stake?

"I'll do what I can, whatever I can. If there is nothing that I can do, then at least I will be with my family and I will share their fate with them." Her words were calm. She made up her mind. There was no other way.

"I see." Lord Faust seemed intrigued. He got of his chair and went toward the cupboard in the corner of the room. "Well, maybe you can't fight, but you can still be of some use."

He opened and closed several drawers before he found what he was looking for. He turned toward Sitheia and handed her a pouch.

"I know that you've been studying with Agnes, the Alchemist. These are some healing salves. With your rudimentary knowledge of healing, you should be able to use them. They are meant for surface injuries and smaller cuts. They should come in handy."

"Thank you." Sitheia said taking the pouch and

putting it in her backpack. "How do you know that I've been studying alchemy?"

Lord Faust smiled smugly.

"Sitheia, my dear. It is my job to know every single thing about Sacred Pools and its inhabitants. How swimming in the enchanted pool went?" He said making Sitheia blush. "It is no wonder that you had such a reaction to the water. Regular Cat people don't have the defense mechanism that is natural for all priests."

Sitheia lowered her head to hide her blushing face. Does he know about Katherine? He probably does. He seems to know everything.

Leading her back to her horse, Lord Faust was mostly quiet. When she got up on the horse, he held the reins for a moment.

"Sitheia? Please do me a favor." He said without any trace of the previous smugness.

"Of course." She said surprised that an emissary is asking for a favor when he can just order her whatever he wanted from her.

"Don't get yourself killed. I put a lot of work and a lot more at stake to create you. Please, don't let it all go to waste." He said letting go of the reins.

Sitheia nodded absentmindedly. That "created" that he used poked her brain, but she didn't have the time to examine the meaning of it. She checked that she has everything with her, the backpack, the bow with arrows and the healing salves. Sitheia was as ready as she was ever going to be. She nudged the horse forward and she was off.

CHAPTER 18

As soon as the horse started moving, a feeling of dread overtook her. She was scared that someone she knew might get killed. Sitheia bit her lip to chase away the thought that someone from her family might get hurt.

She didn't know what to do, but she sure didn't want to wait here. In her entire life she has never faced even the thought that one day she may be involved in violent events. Nothing bad ever happened in Sacred Pools. The Cat people were peaceful folk, who weren't even capable of violence according to her grandfather.

Mrs. Agnes said that the Cat villages were so well hidden that it was almost impossible for someone to find them. So no, she was not prepared for this. None of her people were.

Sitheia had to get back. She had to try, and if she can't help… Then at least she'll be with her family and she'll share in the fate of her people.

For someone who has never ridden a horse, she was doing very well. Her instincts were telling her how to steer the horse and how not to fall off him. She got near the village rather fast. The voices coming from Sacred Pools announced its dire circumstances long before she even had the village in sight. Her heart skipped a beat when she heard the voices coming from the village.

Quickly Sitheia dismounted and let the horse graze on its own from the grass near the road. Crouching she got closer. Still under the cover of the trees, she looked over the wheat field and saw smoke coming from several places in the village.

'They are not burning the village, are they?' She thought.

Wild battle cries accompanied by frightened calls for help overwhelmed her senses. Her heart was beating so fast that she didn't dare to get any closer. Screams of terror and savage relish mixed into a dreadful symphony.

'What kind of monsters are these people?' The fear was building up inside her paralyzing her mind.

Sitheia feared for her own safety and for the safety of her family, but she felt stuck in place and unable to move.

It was as if her feet were frozen solid into the ground.

She spotted near the forest two savages with ugly faces engaging a guard. The guard parried every attack or blocked them with his shield. He was clearly more skilled than the two bandits and was keeping them at bay with ease. One of the bandits, the one who was wielding a morning star got impatient and rushed forward striking at the guard with his entire strength. The guard blocked the blow with his shield but he quickly stepped away letting the bandit be carried by his momentum making him lose balance.

The other bandit scared that on his own he wouldn't stand a chance against the guard plunged his sword trying to pierce the guards' belly with the blade. The guard parried the blade with ease and swinged his sword to chop off the bandit's head. Sitheia held her breath waiting for the killing blow to lend, but it never came. The three of them were stunned by what happened. The blade froze in midair. The bandit, who had closed his eyes expecting to die, let out a horrific laugh when he saw what happened.

Sitheia clapped her mouth with both hands desperately trying to keep the screams back, because in the next moment the bandit plunged his sword in the belly of the guard. With a roaring laugh he picked up his buddy and they both ran off toward the village, calling to their brethren about this new turn of events.

Sitheia looked at the fallen guard with blood coming

of his mouth. He was still alive, but he didn't have a lot of time left. He was dying.

Quickly she pulled a healing salve out of her bag and rushed toward the guard keeping herself as low as possible. The healing salve was meant more for surface wounds rather than stab wounds, but if the salve was able to keep him alive for at least an hour or two until a healer gets to him, then it was worth the shot.

The guard was starting to spasm, when she took the entire salve and plunged it in his wound. He didn't scream, only spit out some blood. That made her fear for his life even more. Agnes had told her that the more the wound is serious the less the person can feel the pain. The alchemist told her that it was a way for the brain to protect the body from the wounds that are too severe until the person removes the immediate danger. It was a delaying effect.

Sitheia couldn't tell if the salve was fixing the damage, but she could say that at least the guard wasn't twitching anymore. The guard grabbed her arm and looked at her.

"I had him... The blade stopped... I couldn't..."

"Shh." She put a finger to her mouth. "Don't talk. The salve may buy you some time. You lay here and don't draw attention to yourself. A regiment from the castle will arrive soon. Just hold on."

The guard quieted and closed his eyes. He wasn't dead. She could see the uneven movement of his chest. He just lost consciousness.

Sitheia dived into the wheat field so she won't get noticed. What just happened was gnawing at her thoughts. The curse was real. Her people can't even defend themselves.

'We are sheep to be slaughtered.' She thought. 'They are going to kill us all, long before the castle's army arrives.'

In those moments of despair a strong wind started blowing. That strong and cold wind was unusual for here in the valley. It was just like when she was at her tower. An image of the Door appeared before her eyes and the despair was dissolved. She felt courage and determination to rid her land of this filth.

"Thank you." She whispered to her friend.

Sitheia checked her bow and with a ready arrow she started sneaking forward toward the houses. The yelling and the screaming were not as often as before. Is everyone captured or dead? Not knowing what was going on made her move faster.

CHAPTER 19

Moving through the crops without getting noticed by anyone was easy. All of the bandits have gone inside the village already. Sitheia tried not to think about what she was going to do once she gets to the village.

Sitheia made up a simple and hopefully good plan. She needed to get into the village undetected. Then she was to find a tall building from where she will be able to see what the situation was. Her primary goal was to try to get her family to hide. If she can't do that, then Sitheia intended to join them and wait for the regiment to arrive without drawing attention to herself or her family.

Sitheia needed to cross the bridge in order to enter the village. There was another bridge near the temple further to the east. But going to the other bridge was going to take too much time and Sitheia didn't know if the other bridge was better guarded than this one. There was a small clearing of open land where the road that came from the sea connected with the bridge.

Right at the bridge she encountered a savage holding a bottle of ale in one hand and a Cat woman in the other. Sitheia recognized the woman. She wasn't sure about her name, but she has seen her in the village and now she was in jeopardy.

The bandit was dragging her by the hair. She tried to resist, but her hands froze in midair every time she tried to hit the bandit or scratch at his face.

In the blink of an eye, Sitheia had an arrow pointed at the bandit. She could feel the point in his neck where the arrow was going to hit. She held her breath and knew that when she releases her breath, the arrow will fly into that savage. 'Will it?' She thought. 'Or will it stop in midair?' Sitheia didn't know what the outcome was going to be and she didn't want to risk missing, so she stayed her hand.

With trembling hands Sitheia lowered her bow. She didn't want to think of what was going to happen to the woman. Because if she allowed herself to think like that, she was going to fall apart right there and she couldn't afford that luxury now. Not while she had no idea if her family was safe. She hated it, but with the curse over her people, she couldn't do anything to stop it.

The bandit dragged the woman across the bridge wanting to have her without needing to share his prey with his buddies. This unfortunate situation gave Sitheia the opportunity to sneak close to the bridge. She was almost crawling in order to remain unseen, but she managed to get across the river and hide herself in the bushes that were in the backyard of the first house next to the bridge.

Since the Inn was the tallest building in the village beside the home of the Village Elder and was so close, Sitheia decided to go there. She wanted to see what was going on in the village and possibly to locate her family.

As she was sneaking through the shadows close to hedges and house corners, she was very careful because the sun was still not gone for the day. If the bandits were to see her, she would be caught. From the time when she worked at the Inn, Sitheia knew that there was a back entrance. She reasoned that there will be a lot of people in front of the main entrance, so she didn't even try to go that way.

Sneaking toward the back entrance was a lot easier. She heard a lot of voices coming from inside the Inn, but she encountered no one near the back. Sitheia assumed that the bandits were not inside the Inn looking for a bed to sleep. If they were looking to plunder the storage, then they would be looking from the back entrance a little further to the right. They would probably also want to get to the barrels of ale that were in the cellar. That was further to the left down the stairs. It was her belief that taking the stairs to the second floor on the left side of the entrance would be the safest route.

Carefully, she sneaked in through the backdoor and up the stairs. Her heart almost stopped when a loose floorboard on the stairs creaked. Thank the Goddess. There was no one nearby to hear it.

On the second floor the doors to every room were opened and all the rooms were trashed. The bandits obviously haven't found anything of value, so on the entire floor there was no one left. Sitheia knew that at the far end of the hallway there was a door to a small balcony overlooking the center of Sacred Pools. She needed to get on that balcony in order to try to locate her family.

On the way to the balcony right after the end of the hallway where it makes a turn, Sitheia heard noise coming from the lower floor. It came from the ventilation grate. Doing her best to be quiet she crouched near the grate and peaked through the tiny holes.

The holes on the grate were too small and she couldn't see much. She saw a lot of people moving, but she couldn't make sense of what was going on downstairs.

"Move your lazy ass stupid cow!" A loud rough voice came from the main floor of the Inn. "I am telling you Ed. I love this place."

"Hey! If you drop the bag, I'll drop you!" Another voice said that seemed like it came from a drunken person. "I know what you mean Ram. It's the best place in the world."

"Yea. Plenty of food. Plenty of ale. And plenty of women. And it's all free." Ed said with a happy voice and with a rougher one he yelled. "Hey, you! No slacking!"

"Ha! I've always wanted to say that to someone else! These poor schmucks can't even defend themselves. It's like taking a candy from a baby." Ram said with a mouth half filled with food.

"How come we've never been here before? All these years of robbing farmers and attacking caravans, we've always had to work our asses off to get a decent score. But, after today we are settled for years."

"It's the Boss. He discovered this place."

"Really?"

"Yea. He is looking for something in here, something valuable."

"Do you know what that 'thing' that he is looking for is? Is it some kind of jewel?"

"No. I think I heard that it was some kind of special girl or something."

"What's so special about this girl?"

"I think that she is a witch or something. She is supposed to be having some kind of weird dreams or visions or something. I don't know."

Sitheia couldn't hear anything else from the deafening noise of her heart pounding in her chest. "They are looking for me. For the girl that has visions. Who else could it be?"

Not feeling strong enough to get up on her feet, she crawled away from the grate tears running down her face. "Is this all my fault? Have all the suffering that my people have been through is because of me?" Sitheia felt as if her throat was closing in and she had difficulty breathing.

An image of the Door flashed before her eyes.

"Thank you." Sitheia whispered.

Her friend has been very helpful today. She still felt the guilt, but she wasn't paralyzed by it anymore. Sitheia knew in her heart that if she was indeed the reason why the village was attacked, then she had to do something about it. The only thing that she was able to do to make up for it was to help protect her people long enough until the army arrives.

CHAPTER 20

Using all of her sneaking abilities so she won't be detected, Sitheia got onto the balcony so she can have a look at her surroundings. No one was looking up because they were all busy on the ground. But still, she didn't want to take an unnecessary risk by lifting her head any higher above the wooden fence. Being precautious has never failed her so far.

Sitheia has lived her entire life in Sacred Pools. She knew more or less every corner of the village, especially its center in front of the Village Elder's home. Looking down she had trouble recognizing the place. Sitheia could see at least five houses that were on fire. She recognized the roof of the house that was owned by a cattle herder that was on fire and smoking.

Nothing looked to be the same as she left it several hours ago. On one side, right in front of the Inn there were maybe a dozen horse drawn carts filled with sacks with everything that the villagers owned. On the carts there were grain, meat, cheese, flour, sugar, clothes, wool, linen, pots and tools, everything that the bandits have found to have some kind of value.

A line of people, Cat people, were moving like ants with sacks loaded on their backs. They moved from the Inn toward the carts, hunched under the weight of the heavy sacks occasionally wincing when a whip would strike at them for being too slow.

The bandits satisfied by their own cruelty watched with pleasure as the peaceful Cat people surrendering all of their belongings. A spark of delight would glow in their evil eyes every time they could find an excuse to use their stinging whips.

Across the street, guarded by more men with swords, the remaining Cat people waited for their fate. The Cat people outnumbered the bandits twenty to one or more, but the damned curse was pacifying them.

Separated from the majority of the people was a group of girls. Sitheia recognized all those girls. It was difficult not to. They were all from her class, just a year or two younger than she was. They all had chains on their hands and around their necks.

'Goddess, please don't let them do that. They are not going to take them away?' Sitheia prayed in her mind.

Between the girls and the rest of the Cat, a man stood and spoke to the villagers. Because of the mixture of sounds, she couldn't understand what he was saying.

Sitheia assumed that he was their leader. Almost all of the bandits wore simple clothes made either from hides or from fur. He was the only one among them that was wearing armor. The armor was similar to hers. It was made of leather. But unlike her armor, his was filthy and darkened by stains of dried blood. Sitheia tried not to think how many people have lost their lives painting his armor with their blood.

Sitheia also noticed that before his feet there was a pile of several bodies of guards that have been murdered during the attack. Behind him on the ground was the Village Elder. From what Sitheia was able to see, he wasn't dead. But, he was badly beaten up. For a man of his age…, Sitheia shuddered from the thought.

Not even in her wildest dreams has she ever imagined being in a situation such as this one. She had no idea what to do. She didn't know how to help her people. Sitheia still had her bow with her and she was a good shot, but she had only seven arrows in total. If she was to fire a single arrow, her defenseless people would be the first to get hurt.

The image of the injured guard from outside the village came to her mind. Even if she fires a single arrow at the head of one bandit, what will she gain? The stupid curse that is paralyzing her people will apply to her as well. Every arrow that she is going to fire will stop in midair, just like that guard's sword did.

It was hopeless. There was nothing that she could do to help. As she sat on the balcony with her arms hugging her knees, Sitheia contemplated her options. Now, all they had to do was to wait for the army to arrive and save at least some of the people. Taking another peak, her eyes spotted her parents. They were standing in the front row. They were squeezing into each other so they can hide her little sister behind them. Their protectiveness touched her. Grandfather Peter was there with them as well. She wanted so much to protect her family.

Her heart sank. She couldn't stay here while her family is in jeopardy. Perhaps there is nothing that she can do to fight off the bandits. But at least, if she is down there with them, she will share in their fate. No matter what that fate turns out to be like.

With resignation, Sitheia removed her quiver and together with her bow she propped them in the corner of the balcony. Keeping herself low, she sneaked out of the Inn and started moving through the backyards and near the fences circling until she got on the opposite side of the

Inn, close to where the Cat people were gathered.

Moving unnoticed took some time. Looking at the sky that started to go dark, Sitheia hoped that the regiment from Castle Perdival will arrive soon. She noticed that torches were lit around the center. By this time of the day usually there were a lot more torches and lanterns than this.

There was no point in delaying any longer. She stood up feeling a little strange being upright after hours of sneaking around. Looking at herself she noticed how much dirt there was over her armor. She tried to dust it off a bit, but it still looked just like any other peasants outfit.

Lifting her chin up, Sitheia did her best to give the appearance that she was brave even though she wanted nothing more than to be anywhere else but here. As she moved toward the place where her family was standing, Sitheia whispered a prayer to the Goddess asking that all of her family would see the next sunrise.

Before entering the crowd, Sitheia got a glimpse of the people that were loading the carts. A skinnier man wasn't able to bear the weight of the heavy sack any longer and he dropped it on the street spilling grains everywhere. The two men that were guarding the carts jumped on him immediately and started kicking the exhausted peasant.

"Stupid animal! Look what you did! That is food that you just spilled on the street!"

"You have so much, that you don't care if one bag is

spilled, don't you? You want us to eat it from the ground like animals? Is that what you think we are?"

"If you can't carry sacks, then what good are you for?"

Kicking and cursing at the defenseless man made Sitheia's fear disappear instantaneously being replaced by anger and hatred toward these vicious animals that are violating the peaceful nature of these people.

She clenched her fists so hard that her nails dig into her skin drawing drops of blood. Sitheia forced herself to move into the crowd and avoid doing something that she would regret for a very short time because she would be dead soon after.

Getting closer to the gathered people, Sitheia was finally able to hear what the man that she saw from the balcony was yelling at the gathered Cat.

"There is no need for more of your people to die! If we have to kill you, we will! We don't care about your lives! They are nothing to us! We will kill every men, women and child in this stink hole that you call a village! But, there's no need for that! That would be just too much work for us!" As Sitheia was slowly getting closer to where her family was, the voice of the man yelling was getting louder. "Give us what we want and we will leave you alone! I promise! We don't want to waste our time here! It's boring! And if we are bored, then we would be needing some entertainment! And that is not good for you! Gold, flour, meat! Pile it all on the wagons and we will be off! You won't be seeing us again! You have my word! Ha, ha, ha!"

The rough savage voice was flooding the villagers with fear. Sitheia already was able to see the back of her family's heads, but the crowd was getting ticker and ticker the closer she got to the street and the bandits. She didn't wanted to, but she had to do some shoving and pushing people aside so she can get near her family. The Cat people that she encountered on her way were more than eager to step aside for her, happy to be further away from the trouble.

When she got close enough to her family, she touched her parents' hands from behind hoping that they won't get startled. They turned a little and a relief spread over their faces when they saw her. Tears flowed down Mary's face. Sitheia was relieved that they both remained silent. Unfortunately, when little Dana saw her sister a small sound of happiness escaped her mouth.

It was Sitheia's misfortune that the bandit that was doing the yelling just a moment ago heard Dana and looked in their direction. His eyes fell on Sitheia and an ugly smile spread over his face.

"Now, look what we have here!" He said grabbing for Sitheia's elbow and pulling her forward in front of the crowd. "You are a pretty little thing, are you? You haven't been hiding from us? You know, you look to be exactly the age that we've been looking for."

He cupped her jaw looking at her face. Sitheia spit at him and he backhanded her. Her head rocked back and her lip started bleeding. She has gotten herself injured growing up many times and in so many different ways on her 'adventures', but she has never been hit by another human being before. That experience was new to her and it was a shock.

"You need to learn some manners. If you are not the girl that the Boss is searching for, then you'll fetch a nice price in Rockfell." He said patting her cheek.

Sitheia has never been so scared and nauseated at the same time. The man that held her elbow stank so badly, that she gagged thinking that she might vomit. But then Peter Cat, her grandfather stepped up from the crowd.

"Leave my granddaughter alone! You took everything from us! Wasn't that enough? Don't you people have a consciousness?" He said breathing heavily.

The bandit got confused for a moment, clearly surprised by the courage of Peter, but he recovered quickly. He let go of Sitheia and approached the old man with a menacing smile.

"Oh, is she your granddaughter. Well, I'll be damned. I didn't know that. Did anyone knew that and forgot to tell me? That she is his granddaughter? Did you?" He mockingly asked one of the bandits that was standing nearby, who shook his head in response. "No? Well, that changes everything. We should just pack up and leave, then." He said turning toward Peter and he plunged his dagger into the old man's chest.

The last rays of sunlight disappeared behind the hill making her grandpa's blood look black like tar. Witnessing this was worse than seeing the guard being stubbed. The last expression of her grandfather was a look of surprise and fear on his face that seared into her mind. The pain of the loss was burning away at bonds she didn't know that she had.

The image of the Door appeared before her eyes urging her forward. A scream of primal anguish and rage tore from her throat. It sounded nothing like her voice. Nothing like a human should sound like.

The next moment, Sitheia flung herself in the air like a cat and jumped in the bandit's embrace. Her tiny dagger was suddenly in her hand answering her call and she started stabbing the neck of the vile creature. The blade pierced the tender flesh of the neck with ease and tore at blood vessels and muscles and throat. Blood spurted over her face and she felt a strange mixture of calm satisfaction and exhilaration for ending the life of the person who stole her grandpa from her.

Sitheia pulled the bloody dagger and stabbed again and kept repeating the motion while screaming her lungs out. Her act of savagery stunned everyone and no one moved or reacted in any way until she stopped moving over the bloody mess that until a moment ago was the leader of the bandits.

But, soon the bandits came to their senses and called out angry battle cries.

"Kill that wench!" They called out and ran after her.

In the blink of an eye Sitheia was on her feet and running faster than she ever had. Her life literally depended on her not getting caught. She fell and got up with scratched hands, but she continued to run without looking back until she reached the bridge and could run no more. Her legs failed her. Falling down, she saw her pursuers getting closer.

Seeing that she was on the ground, they slowed down with ugly smiles that promised nothing good.

"End of the line little chicken."

Sitheia was certain that it was over, her life was about to end, probably in a very unpleasant way. She pushed herself to her feet not wanting to die kneeling in the dirt. With the tiny bloody dagger still clutched in her hand she looked at them and in that moment she hated them as she has never known hate before.

Looking at the changed expression on her face the bandits stopped for a moment, before discarding her expression of savagery and hatred as a bluff. They moved forward brandishing their weapons.

With all the strength that she had left, she forced her legs to move forward intending to attack the bandits herself. She focused herself on the closest bandit and readied herself for the fight that probably would result with her death. 'At least I will go down fighting back and not cowering under the bed.' She thought.

Before the bandit could close on the last several steps that were between the two of them, an arrow pierced his left eye. Sitheia blinked thinking that she was imagining things as a result of the stress, fear and exhaustion. But, by the reaction of the other bandits, she concluded that it really happened and she wasn't imagining anything.

A second arrow found home in the chest of another bandit. The third bandit burst into flames leaving nothing but ash behind.

"Run for your lives!" One of the bandits screamed and turned to run back toward the village.

Before his words died down, he fell on the ground struck by lightning. Sitheia looked behind her and saw a large number of armed men and women. She also saw arrows and flames flying toward the bandits.

The rest of the bandits turned as well and started running in the opposite direction, back toward the village. A large ball of fire hit one bandit in the back and exploded. The explosion caught four more men who fell on the ground clutching their scorched body parts. Several more arrows found home in the backs of more bandits.

One bandit froze solid while he was in the process of jumping over the corpse of one of his fallen brothers and shuttered into many small pieces of frozen meat when he finally reached the ground. A strong wind bellowed past Sitheia and knocked the rest of the bandits of their feet.

"Charge!" She heard being yelled from behind her back followed by a two dozen heavily armed riders who swooped down from behind Sitheia and descended on the remaining bandits.

Sitheia was overwhelmed by the ferocity with which the Perdivals fought. Their movements were swift, precise and unbelievably strong. When one of the Perdivals would swing a sword a bandits' head would fall off or a bandit would be cut in two. Not being able to take it anymore, Sitheia buckled over and throw up.

Whipping her mouth from her sleeve she looked around. All the bandits in sight were dead and groups of Perdival riders were already on the hunt for any strugglers. The regiment from Perdival castle has arrived in time to save her life. It was over. The village was saved. All those girls in chains were saved. Only her grandpa was not saved. It was too late for him. Sitheia fell on her knees where she stood and clutched her face with both hands.

She couldn't believe what just happened. What twisted fate made these events real? How could this have happened?

In her entire life, no bandit has ever been spotted near the village. Their village was supposed to be hidden so that no one could find its way to them. But somehow, these bandits have succeeded in discovering the village and they have come to murder her grandfather. How?

And she has taken a life. She looked at her hands covered with dark sticky almost dried blood. She has taken a life. How is that possible? She shouldn't be able to… She is a Cat. She should be cursed. A Cat should not be able to harm anyone, let alone kill someone. Now, Sitheia really did felt like she was cursed.

All these emotions overwhelmed her. All that fear mixed with grief and hatred toward those vile men who have desecrated their peaceful homes. As she sat there in the dirt, a stream of tears tried to take with them some of the abundance of emotions that she had with them.

"Are you all right?" A voice came from behind her.

She turned to look at the person that was speaking to her. It was Prince Marcus, the blond emissary from the castle. He looked genuinely concerned for her safety. Strange, this was the first time that she was in the presence of a Lord of Perdival and she didn't blushed or felt moved at all by his presence. Sitheia did not answer.

The Prince got off his horse and approached her, leading his beast behind.

"They didn't hurt you, did they?" He asked again.

"They killed my grandpa." Sitheia mumbled looking at the Prince hoping that he would tell her that she is wrong and that her grandpa is alive. That didn't happen.

"I am sorry. We came as fast as we could."

"Sitty! Sitty!" Her parents' frightened cries pulled her attention from the Prince.

Her parents came running calling her name with Dana running close after them. When they saw her they stopped in their tracks mortified by her appearance. Her sister started crying when she saw Sitheia. Then George and Mary both embraced their daughter crumbling together on their knees and they started checking her body for injuries.

"Are you hurt?" George asked looking for wounds.

"Where does it hurt, child?" Mary said looking at her daughter's eyes pushing her matted hair from her face.

"I am not injured." Sitheia said and looked at herself.

Her armor was drenched in the blood of the bandit. She guessed that her face was probably a bloody mess too and that her appearance might be scary. Her mother took out a handkerchief and tried to clean the blood from her face, but the white handkerchief got soaked with blood in a moment without cleaning anything.

"There is so much blood on you." Her mother said, trying to clean her daughter as if that way she may undo the horror of what just happened.

Sitheia didn't try to stop her parents. Her mind was on

her blade plunged into the neck of the bandit.

"I killed him." She whispered, but they all heard her. Her parents froze, Dana shuddered and the Prince leaned in closer. "I killed him."

"It's all right." Her parents hugged her while she cried in their arms.

Sitheia didn't hold back. All the emotions that have piled up inside her were coming out and she let the tears flow like waterfalls. Another pair of smaller hands joined the hug and she felt slightly better knowing that her sister is safe. Finally, after a very long day Sitheia allowed herself to slump in the arms of her family.

With her teary eyes closed and her mind relaxing, Sitheia suddenly felt something that she has never felt before. She felt as if the consciousness of someone else touched her mind. Her instincts made her open her eyes and jumped on her feet startling everyone, including the Prince.

She felt like something was pulling her toward the center of the village where her grandfather was killed.

"Sitty? What's wrong?"

Without paying attention to anyone around her, she started walking and then she was running at full speed. Sitheia could not explain what was happening because it has never happened before. But, she felt that something terrible was happening right now. And she knew that she has to go and do something before it was too late. Sitheia felt as if a part of her was dying. She was terrified, but she was determined not to lose anyone else today.

Even before she arrived at her destination she had the feeling who was the person that she was going to find lying in a pool of his own blood.

Her special friend Katherine was kneeling next to a large blond man. It was John, her John. His face was ashen grey and strained from the pain. The blond hair was matted and filthy. On the left side of his belly there was a huge red stain. Sitheia couldn't say a word. She just dropped on her knees next to him. There was a bad smell coming from the wound like from a toilet.

"I am sorry. I tried to heal him, but he is too far gone. I am not that powerful healer. I don't know how or if it is even possible at this stage." Katherine said with heavy voice. "When you killed that man... And they started chasing you. He went after the men that were pursuing you and he tackled one of them. He started punching him in the face. He didn't even see the other bandit... He came from behind... He stubbed him..."

Sitheia was trying to take in what she was seeing, but her brain refused to let her accept that most likely she was going to lose John too. Something nudged at her hand. It was Miss. Olivia, Mrs. Agnes's cat. When Sitheia didn't respond to her sniffing, she moved closer to John.

Katherine shooed her away when the cat started lapping the blood that has pooled up around John. Miss. Olivia hissed toward the acolyte, before she ran off.

"No." Sitheia said refusing to accept this reality. She wrinkled her nose at the smell.

"I think that the sword tore his guts." Katherine said.

"No! You are not dying too!" She said louder while looking at his face.

John was looking at her. The pain was gone from his face. He was looking at her with a smile and something inside her told her that it was not a good sign.

"No, no, no, no! I will not let you die! I won't!" Sitheia yelled out loud.

The numbness that she felt when she first saw him lying there was evaporating. In its place, rage and fury filled her heart. Driven by the urgency and the connection that she had with John, she put both hands on his body pressing at the wound.

"It won't stop the bleeding. I tried." Katherine said misunderstanding her intentions.

John has sworn allegiance to her merely hours ago. He was her responsibility. If he can only take some of her own life, then she might be able to save him. She didn't want to pray again to the Goddess. She already prayed that her entire family survives the day, but her grandpa was dead and now John was dying too. The Goddess would not help her. She had to find a way herself.

Sitheia started to feel dizzy and her heart was burning so hot she feared that her chest will burst into flames. She loved John. Not as a girl loves a boy, but as something more. Like a parent loving a child. He was hers. She needed him as much as he needed her.

Sitheia felt blinded by the vortex of her emotions. It was so bright until she realized that it was not her emotions that were blinding her but the bright light coming from her hands. Light that could equal the sun. She became oblivious to the world around her. She couldn't hear or see anyone. And when the light finally disappeared, darkness fell over her.

CHAPTER 21

Sitheia woke up several hours later in a strange room that she didn't recognized. She was lying on a strange bed that was higher from the ground than any other bed that she has ever seen. By the amount of noise that was coming from every direction, Sitheia could tell that there were a lot of people in the room or hall or whatever that place was.

Her first thought was 'Not another dream.'

She noticed that her family was standing nearby next to a wall. Her grandpa was not with them, of course. The sting of that thought made her clench her fists and she realized that she couldn't. Her right hand was so heavily bandaged that she couldn't move any of her fingers at all.

"Look. She is awake." Sitheia heard Dana's voice.

In the blink of an eye, the bed where she was lying got surrounded by her family.

"It's all right dear. You are all right." Mary said.

"Don't try to move your hand." George said. "There was a cut on your palm. Agnes put some cream on it, but said that you shouldn't move it at least one week or it will leave a scar."

Sitheia looked at her hand. It was wrapped with so much linen that it reminded her of the way her people used to wrap the dead bodies of their relatives to preserve them when they used to lay the dead to rest in the catacombs. That was in ancient times. Thinking about dead bodies made her remember the last thing that she was doing before she blacked out.

"John!" Sitheia said loudly, raising into a sitting position a bit too fast. Her parents put a hand on her shoulders to steady her.

"Easy. Relax, and speak a little quieter. We are not alone here and you are not fully recovered yet." Her father said.

Sitheia looked around and saw that there were at least half a dozen more beds just like hers. Around most there were gathered people of family members who were waiting for some member of their family to recover.

"He's alive." Her mother said giving a small smile that made her take an easier breath.

"You saved him." Dana said proud of her big sister. "Lady Zorra said that you made a miracle."

"Who is Lady Zorra?"

"She is a…" Dana started to answer, but she couldn't find the words to explain.

"Lady Zorra is an emissary from Castle Perdival." Mary said.

"She is a very powerful and a very skilled healer." George said. "We owe her a lot."

Sitheia rubbed her head with her healthy hand trying to put her thoughts in order.

"What happened? The last I remember was: I was kneeling next to John and he was dying. Is he really OK?" The worried girl asked as her parents exchanged looks as if they were communicating with their eyes and it pissed her off because she was excluded from the conversation. "Tell me the true! What happened?"

"Honey, we didn't really saw what happened." Mary said carefully as if she was talking to a mentally unstable person that might go off at any moment. "When you just got up and ran back toward the center of the village, we didn't know what was going on. So we just followed you. And when we finally caught up with you, we saw you glowing so bright it was like looking at the sun."

"I was glowing?"

"I have never even heard of something like that being

done, ever." George said rubbing his brow. Sitheia noticed that his hair looked grayer than usual. "And when the light disappeared, you fell on the ground unconscious."

"What about John? Is he all right? Is he going to survive?" None of their answers addressed her concern. What was happening with John? She needed to know.

"When Lady Zorra came and saw the two of you unconscious, she examined both of you. You were exhausted. You were drained from almost all of your life force." George said. "And she couldn't find anything wrong with John. There was no sign on him that he was ever injured. He was fully healed."

Sitheia let go of her breath in relief. He was OK. A small tired smile spread over her face.

"The healers are keeping him under observation. They can't explain how you managed to do that." Mary said. "You've never had any magical or healing training. And Lady Zorra said that even a fully trained healer wouldn't be able to heal that much damage in that short of time. She said that the fear and the excitement of everything that happened today may have given you the emotional help to do what normally would be much more difficult to achieve."

"Sitty. You have never done magic before, have you?" Her father asked.

"Never." Sitheia said right away. She thought of the

connection that she has created with John and Katherine, but that was her business and she didn't want to share that information with anyone.

"Well, we both have people with magical abilities in our bloodlines." George said. "I thought that Faith was the last one, but I guess you have inherited some of her gifts and maybe some more."

Sitheia didn't know what to think about being able to do magic, and potentially being a healer. Her heart was telling her that it was more because of her connection to John that she was able to help him and not because of some magic inside her that just now happened to appear out of nowhere.

Sitheia didn't manage to see this Lady Zorra, but Mrs. Agnes came to see her. After a quick examination she declared that Sitheia was cleared to go home. They did not let her see John telling her that he was still recovering, but she will be able to see him the next day.

Exiting the building where the injured were being treated, Sitheia noticed that the villagers have lit up the entire area with torches and lanterns. Her parents informed her that the regiment from Perdival Castle has performed a sweep through the village and the woods to look for any strugglers. After a sorcerer from the regiment has performed a magical scan on the area for any intruders it has been declared that the bandits have been destroyed entirely.

During the attack, seven guards have been killed and fourteen were wounded. Four other Cat have been killed when they have tried unsuccessfully to prevent the bandits from entering their homes. Many dozens of Cat were injured in the attack. The Lords of Perdival have set up a triage tents and they have converted some old building like the one that Sitheia has just walked out of into a place to medicate all wounded. There were a lot of bruises and cuts that were easier to take care off. The Alchemist Agnes was a great help with her potions for those.

The Village Elder was beat up pretty badly and he needed a lot of attention. Agnes was good with her potions, but for the broken arm and broken ribs she could do nothing. Thankfully the mysterious Lady Zorra proved to be very skilled with healing spells so she helped mending the bigger injuries, leaving the smaller to heal on their own.

By morning the tending of the wounded was finished. Some smaller injuries have remained untreated and were left to be taken care of after the healers had some rest. All the fires have been put out. Several buildings have been burned to the ground, but the people who lived there were taken in by their neighbors or relatives.

Fixing the damaged buildings and rebuilding those that were completely destroyed was going to start tomorrow and it was going to take some time. But, the Cat were a people that helped each other and they were going to help each other with the rebuilding project as well. The next important thing that needed to be done now, was to take care of their dead.

This entire time Sitheia have been shuffled around not being able to tell head or tail of what was going on. You go there, no go over there. Do this, now do that. Say "Ahh". Does this hurt? What about now? Lady Zorra and Agnes examined her several times. After they determined that from all the blood that was on her armor, none of it belonged to her, they started looking for any head injuries or concussions or whatever they call them. Sitheia kept telling them that she was all right and she demanded to see John. Finally they caved in.

She found him sleeping in a medical tent. He had no shirt and there was a large bandage over his torso. Sitheia sat there next to him careful not to wake him and just watched him sleep for a while.

Agnes gave her a potion to calm her nerves which didn't help. It only made her head feel light like it was floating. Prince Marcus himself came to check in on her several times. Sitheia caught him looking at her with an unnerving look. She pretended that she wasn't noticing it, but that unnerving look was sent in her direction very often over the last day.

Bandaged almost from head to toes, the Village Elder gathered many important villagers, few at a time and had at least thirty meetings within twenty four hours. George attended three of those. When he returned home he said that the Village Elder was concerned about providing shelter and food for everyone and restoring Sacred Pools to its normal way of life.

The major concern was how the bandits were even able to find the village. Representatives from the castle have taken upon themselves to discover the flaw in their protection plan and to fix it. George said that there have been plans made to restore the damaged homes so their inhabitants can return to live inside them. He also said that several families have been left without anyone that is capable of supporting them. George said that the Lords of Perdival have taken full responsibility over the care for these families until the children come of age and are able to take care of themselves.

While her parents joined the others in trying to restore order in the village, her sister Dana did not let go of her arm. Someone suggested that she might want to change her clothes, she refused. Someone suggested that at least she should wash the blood from her face, she accepted. Abandoning all forms of civility Sitheia plunged her head in the bucket with cold water that she pulled from the well. The water turned red from the blood on her face.

When she looked around, she noticed that her fellow villagers were keeping their distance from her. Her leather armor has been covered in blood and by now large portions of it have changed to a darker color. She couldn't understand why the people of Sacred Pools were avoiding her, but she didn't really care, at least not right now.

"I think that they are afraid of you." Her sister told her when they were alone.

"I don't understand. Why would they be afraid of me?" Sitheia asked looking at Dana.

"You killed that man." The girl whispered.

"I did it for grandpa, not because I wanted." Sitheia said with a higher voice. She didn't want to believe that the people whom she knew her entire life were punishing her for protecting herself. She looked at her sister with worried look. "You are not afraid of me, are you?"

"No, I am not." Dana shook her head. "If anything happens, I know that you can protect me."

That answer did not bring the comfort that Sitheia was hoping for. Instead it made her even more anxious. Neither she nor the rest of Sacred Pools could ignore what happened. She took a life. She intentionally hurt someone. Sitheia saw it with her own eyes what happens when someone from her village tries to hurt someone. Yet, she did it. She wanted to consider the possibility that somehow the curse broke. But, her sister Dana ended that hope.

"Maybe when that man killed grandpa, the curse broke." Sitheia said hopefully.

"I don't think so." Dana responded. "When you ran with the bandits going after you, dad grabbed a bow and he fired an arrow at one of the bandits. I saw the arrow froze in midair for few seconds before it fell on the ground."

"But, John tackled somebody and he was punching him before he was stubbed. And how was I able to do what I did? How was John able to do that as well?" Sitheia asked the questions that everyone in the village were thinking.

"I don't know. I think I heard someone called it an anomaly. Anyway, I am glad that you did." Dana said with tears running down her face. "That evil man killed grandpa, he deserved to die."

During the funeral Sitheia found herself reliving the memories of what happened to her grandpa and the event after. The whole family huddled together and tried to console one another. It didn't help much, but at least they were together. A girl of four and a boy of eleven got orphaned during the attack. They both lost their parents in the first moments of the attack. Both children held an emissary by their hands.

"They will take them to the castle. They are too young to fend for themselves." George said.

Many emissaries came to the funerals to express their condolences. Sitheia felt as if they were all giving her strange looks.

'At least they look to be curious rather than scared.'

Sitheia thought.

When the crowd started to thin out, a man that was being led by a young woman approached them. He seemed to have been injured and the woman was helping him walk.

"Sitheia?" The man made an effort to speak. Sitheia recognized him as the guard that she tried to help with a healing salve. "My name is Lawson. You saved my life."

"I am relieved to see that you have survived." She said honestly.

"It's all thanks to you. If you weren't there to help, I would have died… Thank you…"

"We both thank you. We learned a week ago that I am pregnant. I am forever in your debt for saving my husband." Said the woman that was helping the man walks.

"Lady Zorra was shocked when she saw the salves inside the wound. She said that the salves slowed down the bleeding. They have saved my life long enough so she can get to me. With Agnes and some other healer they worked for hours on healing the wound. The rest, they said will have to heal on its own. I am forever in your debt."

After the funeral, Sitheia went home with her family wondering how things will ever get back to normal. Looking at the empty chair near the fireplace where her grandpa had the habit of dozing or would gather everyone to tell them stories, it made her feel nauseous again.

A knock at the door broke through her grieving. Her

father opened the door and quickly bowed his head and stepped back.

"Good evening Lord Gavin. Do you require my assistance?" He asked.

"No, George. Not this time. In fact we are here to see your daughter." Lord Gavin said stepping inside followed by Lady Erika and Prince Marcus.

George and Mary looked at them with opened mouths, not understanding what they want with their daughter.

"Don't worry, everything is fine." Lady Erika stepped in.

Lord Gavin turned toward Sitheia with a small smile. Dana clutched her sister's arm from behind her.

"Hello, Sitheia. It's been a while since our meeting at your birthday."

She did not respond, all she could do was stare at him. She wasn't blushing this time, her body and her emotions were too tired for that.

"We've heard that you were very brave during the attack." Lord Gavin continued slowly as if trying not to spook her. "I don't remember ever hearing of a Cat who did what you have done."

Sitheia didn't respond again, but felt that her throat was getting dry. She didn't like where the conversation or more appropriate where the monolog was heading.

"I regret to say that the people of Sacred Pools are

concerned and so are we." He said. "What you did, is not natural to them. And they are worried that you no longer belong in this village. They fear that you may bring more danger to them. We, at Castle Perdival, also agree that there is something different in you."

Her parents couldn't say a word to their masters. They covered their mouths to keep themselves from crying out loud.

'This is it. They are going to banish me from the village.' Sitheia thought. For some reason she didn't feel scared or worried. She felt cold and distant, as if she was back at the tower. Probably that is where she will go to live if they banish her.

"Are you here to banish me?" She asked looking Lord Gavin in the eyes. Again she saw that nervous twitch in them.

The three emissaries shifted in their spots. No Cat has ever before questioned a Lord of Perdival. But, no Cat has ever killed a person also. Lord Gavin regained his composure.

"To banish you? Why would you even think of something like that?" He said with a forced laugh that didn't last long. "We do not abandon our people. We won't abandon you either."

"I don't understand." She said with resignation.

"Your unusual situation has made a very dangerous

question that we must find an answer to it. You being able to kill a man may bring more damage to all of us, than any of us can fathom. I can easily say that your action can be the cause or a symptom that the contract between our people is in danger. And we have to do everything that we can to preserve that contract. Don't you agree?"

Sitheia only nodded without saying anything and Lord Gavin took that as an agreement.

"Good. Regardless of this new turn of events. We have been watching your progress for some time Sitheia Cat. We know that you are a fine trader. You have started to learn how to brew potions. You are also a hunter and now it seems like you have the talent to heal as well. You lack patience, but you'll learn."

"What are you talking about?" Sitheia was confused by what she was hearing.

"Tomorrow, we will take you to your new home. In Sacred Pools you have learned the basics. At the castle we will teach you how to master those skills. I have no doubt that very soon you will be able to put your skills to use. A new and very interesting life awaits you Sitheia. A lot of hard work, but also a lot of rewards will follow as a result. You have until tomorrow at dusk to say your goodbyes. We will wait for you at the bridge to take you to your new home. Have a good evening. Mary, George."

With that the emissaries wore gone through the door

leaving the confused Sitheia to be congratulated by her family. Her mother started to cry.

"I am so proud of you, baby." Her mother was hugging her.

"Our daughter will go to live at the castle." Her father proudly kissed her forehead.

Her sister didn't say anything until it came time to go to bed.

"Am I ever going to see you again?" She asked.

"I don't know. I think so. I don't know. Every convoy that goes to the castle passes from here." Sitheia tried to comfort her little sister.

"I'll miss you."

"I'll miss you too."

When everyone was asleep, Sitheia sneaked out of the house. Her instincts told her to keep herself out of sight. She took no detours and head straight for the hill where she started climbing.

Since she saw the bandits approaching the village she hasn't seen her friend. She missed the Door badly. Especially now she needed the comforting presence of her silent friend. So many things have happened in such a short period of time. Sitheia hated the bandits for attacking her village, for killing her grandfather, for making her feel unsafe in her village where nothing bad ever happened.

She was pissed, but she didn't want to cry. She didn't

want to feel weak. Sitheia wasn't weak when she killed the man who stole her grandfather from her. Yet, if she has only killed the bandit first, then her grandpa would still be alive. She shook her head. Her mind was getting dizzy from all these weird thoughts.

She looked at the Door. For her entire life she spoke to her. The Door knew all her thoughts, all her secrets. Not that she had secrets that wore worth keeping, except the one about her friendship with the Door, of course. And now, Sitheia was chosen to leave her family and her friend behind and to start a new life in service to the Lords of Perdival. Her parents were so proud, but at this moment among all the jumble of emotions that swirled inside of her, mostly she felt lonely. Tomorrow Sitheia will go and she won't have even her silent friend.

"I'll miss you." She whispered as she traced with her finger the ancient carvings on the door.

She made a sob. What did she expected, for the Door to say that she will miss Sitheia too? She has never spoken before, why would she break the silence now?

"Ouch."

Sitheia cut her finger on the edge of a carving. She looked at the Door suspiciously.

"Are you telling me that you are going to miss me too, or that you don't care about me?"

The drop of blood her finger left on the carvings of

the Door disappeared into the wood. The Door shock and swung open.

Sitheia was speechless. That Door hasn't opened in hundreds of years, for anyone. Sitheia has heard stories of people through the ages trying to hack her to pieces, trying to bring it down with a battering ram or set it on fire without success.

But now, it stood open, for her, for a friend.

"So you do care." Sitheia whispered and stepped forward over the threshold.

The room was small, only a few dozen square feet. Half a dozen torches lit up on their own illuminating a lonely metal pedestal in the middle of the room surrounded by candlesticks with thin violet candles. There was nothing else inside the room, neither window nor another door.

As Sitheia got closer to the pedestal, the violet candles lit up on their own. There was something on top of the pedestal. A ring. It was brown and simple, made of wood and very unattractive.

"Is this for me?" Sitheia asked.

As a response, several rows of strange markings started to glow in circles around the pedestal. If that was the language that the Door spoke, Sitheia couldn't understand anything from it. In fact, the markings looked more to Sitheia like chicken scratching than actual words. But, Sitheia didn't need a translation. She knew in her heart that this ring was a gift from a friend and it belonged to her.

"Thank you." She whispered and picked up the ring.

As she left the chamber, the Door closed behind her. When Sitheia looked back at her, it looked exactly the same as it has for hundreds of years. She put the ring in the pouch on her belt, so she won't lose it on her way down. Sitheia looked at her friend with sad eyes for one last time and she went home.

The next day she woke up earlier than usual, she got dressed. She ate in a hurry and went out. Last night before going to sleep she planned the day in a way that she manages to see everyone that mattered to her and say goodbye.

Her first stop was at the temple. After the Goddess failed to keep her family safe, she was not inclined to be friendly with her, but for some reason Katherine was waiting for her in front of the temple.

"I felt that you were coming." Katherine said.

"I wanted to see you. I need to know that you are going to be all right." Sitheia said.

"You are leaving, are you?" Katherine turned her back to hide her face.

"I have to. The Lords of Perdival want to keep an eye on me."

"Because you killed that man?"

"Yes."

"Am I ever going to see you again?" Katherine asked.

Sitheia wanted to say "I don't know" like she did when Dana asked her the same question. But, somehow she knew that she was going to see Katherine again.

"You will." She said and Katherine turned to look at her face. Katherine's eyes were red and streams of tears were flowing from them.

"How do you know?"

"How did you know that I was coming to see you?" Sitheia answered with a question.

"Did you do this to me? What I am feeling for you? Is this is real or is it magic?"

Sitheia considered her question for a moment, before letting her heart give the answer.

"It's both. The connection between us existed before I made the connection stronger with magic." Sitheia said. "Are you mad?"

Katherine did not answer her. Instead she put a hand on the back of her neck and pulled Sitheia in a kiss. When the kiss ended they were both breathing like they have just run a marathon.

"Don't do anything stupid while I am gone." Sitheia said with a happy smile.

"I can't promise that." Katherine returned the smile. "Don't kill anyone while you are gone."

"I also can't promise that." Sitheia answered and they both stopped smiling. "I'll see you as soon as I can."

They exchanged one last shorter kiss before they separated. Katherine entered inside the temple and Sitheia started toward her second stop.

John also was waiting for her in front of his house. It was the first time after the attack that they were together and alone. Sitheia noticed that he was moving with an ease. Guessing her thoughts, John answered them.

"You did a good job. You healed even an old scar that I had that was lagging my left arm a bit. You turned up to be very useful." He said smirking.

"I've heard you were very useful too." Sitheia returned the smirk making his disappear.

"What I did wasn't useful. It was stupid. I just jumped the first guy that I could get to without thinking or even knowing how to fight."

"I think that you were very brave." She said and he gave her a true warm smile.

"I wanted to ask you something, for a favor." John said looking at his feet.

"Sure. What can I do?" Sitheia asked without hesitation.

"Please don't go." He said looking at her eyes with tears running down his cheeks. "Say that you are sick. I'll cover for you. Or let us run away from this place. Just please don't go."

"John, you know I can't do that." Sitheia said with a

lump in her throat.

"I was a nobody when you found me. I will be a nobody again once you leave me." John said with so much pain in his voice that it broke her heart.

"You were never a nobody. You are strong and smart. Sacred Pools should be happy to have you."

"Yea right." He said with a bitter smile.

An idea came to Sitheia's mind.

"I can't predict the future but I know of one thing. I won't be in that castle forever and one day I will need you again." Sitheia said and John looked at her suspiciously to determine if she was only saying that so he can feel better. "When I killed that man, you were the only other Cat that was able to hit someone. Isn't that a little strange?"

"Anomaly. That's what I heard them calling it." John said.

"I think that we were able to fight because of the connection that we share." Sitheia said. "I also heard that you were caught from behind. I think that you need some training."

"What are you saying?" John was confused with what he was hearing.

"While I am at the castle and they are making me master my abilities, I want you to join the guards."

"What?" John asked with the desperation gone from his face.

"You are the only person in Sacred Pools that can defend this place. With me gone, you are the only one for whom the curse does not apply. I have seen a guard fight. They are really good, but the curse is crippling them. I want you to join them and learn from them. Become better at fighting and work on organizing a defense. Because we all saw it, somehow someone may attack again, whether it's bandits or some other enemy. Our people are defenseless and we are their only hope, while we wait for the army to arrive."

John sat quietly contemplating on what he just heard. Sitheia waited patiently for him to finish processing her instructions. At the end he stood up facing her with a fist placed on his heart.

"Your words, I will see them done. I swear to you." He said venerably. They both smiled and Sitheia hugged him.

"We are connected. Even if we are apart, we will always be close to each other." Sitheia said, gave him another hug, kissed him on the cheek and left.

Before she went home, Sitheia said goodbye to several people around the village including the Innkeeper who was still recovering from the attack and to Mrs. Agnes who seemed a little worn out. The cat, Miss. Olivia was nowhere to be seen. She wanted to stay a little longer and talk with the Alchemist. After all she was one of her mentors but, Agnes said that she is not feeling well and wished her luck.

It was strange. But with everything that was happening, Sitheia could easily make a list of things that were normal. It was a shorter list, than what was strange.

Sitheia spent the rest of the day with her family. She had her last dinner. It was a rabbit stew with freshly baked bread. It was the best stew Sitheia ever had. For sure it tasted far better than the rabbit that she has cooked. Even though the food was delicious, it took a lot of effort to swallow even several bites.

Her parents continued to tell her how proud they were. They told her to be brave and that there was nothing to be worried about. She should work hard, make herself useful and she will bring honor to her family.

Sitheia was to go as she was, bringing no personal possessions with her apart for the clothes on her back. She left her bag and her small knife, the same knife she used to kill the bandit. The little pouch where she kept her money, her pendant and the lucky coin that Dana gave it to her for her birthday, had to stay behind too.

As she exchanged goodbyes with her proud parents and her crying sister, Sitheia remembered the little wooden ring which the Door gave it to her that was still lying in the little pouch that she also needed to leave behind.

Sitheia never owned any jewelry, so this little trinket meant a lot to her, especially because it was a gift from the Door. She walked by herself to the meeting place near the bridge, where a dozen emissaries and some other chosen people waited. Feeling that her life would never be the same again she slipped the ring on her finger.

'I am going to a strange place where I don't know a soul. At least, you will be with me.' Sitheia thought.

'Don't worry, friend. I will never leave you.'

EPILOGUE

Well, that would be it, at least for now. Sitheia have started her journey that will make her a legend one day.

I am afraid that I will have to excuse myself for any inaccuracy in my recollection of the events that I recorded in this first volume. The thing is that I wasn't there for this part of her journey. Before I started collecting the information about the events where I wasn't personally involved, I needed to ask for permission to use certain unorthodox methods for gathering information.

I hate to say it, but I was forbidden from using any invasive methods on humans for the purpose of obtaining this information. In other words, I couldn't just see the true for myself in the blood of those that were directly involved.

Instead, I had to actually ask them to volunteer their stories on their own.

There is no doubt that all individuals that were interviewed during my research, did not hesitate to bend the true in their favor. I can personally vouch that at least fifteen percent is true. This, I verified by seeing the true for myself in the blood of the people that were being questioned. Of course, that was before I was forbidden to continue this practice.

As a final note to the first volume in the Legend of Sitheia series, I have to warn all readers. I do not advise them to keep on looking into the history of Sitheia. It is true, her existence was filled with interesting events and on her journey she met some truly remarkable individuals. I count myself honored to be one of them. But, her life story is not for the faint of heart. It is full of darkness and hardship.

If you believe that there is even a small chance that you are squeamish or if you have a weak heart, then it would be better that you stopped reading now.

For the rest, the story about Sitheia will continue in the next volume that is coming soon.

Aristobulus, advisor,
chronicler and historian.

BIOGRAPHY

Vladislav grew up listening to folk and fairy tales. Especially he enjoyed the stories of heroes and villains that came out of myths and legends.

At early age he discovered the infinite world of imagination that came from within books. It was then that he started devouring whole libraries of books. Before he was twenty he has read more than ten thousand books from various genres.

Among his favorite authors are Terry Goodkind and J.R.R. Tolkien.

Vladislav enjoyed the fantasy world of games like Magic the Gathering, Dungeons & Dragons, World of Warcraft and many more.

He discovered that within the power of dreams, lays the creation of infinite worlds each more amazing and more fantastic than the one before.

So, he started telling stories. At first he started telling stories to the people around him and now he finally decided to share his stories with the world.

If you want to get deeper into the story of Sitheia, visit our website www.northstarlegends.com where we will be posting additional information about everything regarding the Legend of Sitheia series.

Artwork, maps, character information, merchandise and also information about the next book that is coming soon, will be available on www.northstarlegends.com.

Your opinion matters to us. So do not hesitate to contact us at legendofsitheia@gmail.com and tell us which parts you liked and which parts you didn't.

We would very much appreciate if you write a review and share your honest opinion about the book. That will help other readers and your feedback will also help us improve. Thank you for purchasing Legacy of the Nameless. We hope that you enjoyed it.